"What's wrong, honey?" asked Mrs. Keenan.

Jamie sighed heavily. "My *former* best friend, Miss Randy Dowell, has decided she likes my worst enemy better than me. Her new best friend is Bill the Pill Baird."

Without waiting for a response, she stomped up the steps and into her room and flung herself down at her desk.

"Okay, Randy," she said between clenched teeth. "If you like Bill the Pill so much, I'm sure you want the whole school to know about it. You said you didn't want to write the column. You said you didn't want the column to be about Bill. Hey, no problem. *I'll* write the column — and it won't be about Bill the Pill, Ran. It'll be about *you*."

#3
Roving Reporter
Elissa Snow

PRICE STERN SLOAN
Los Angeles

Chapter One

"Sugar maples!" shouted Miss Duni.

From her seat in the back of the class-room, Jamie Keenan sighed. Her fourth-grade teacher was at it again.

Everyone at Laughing Egg Elementary School agreed that Miss Duni was a perfect-ly nice teacher, but she had one horrible problem: she got way too excited about things. Jamie could tell that this was about to happen now.

"Sugar maples!" Miss Duni repeated, looking dizzy with excitement. She picked up a maple leaf from her desk and flapped it in the air. Her round glasses bounced up and down on her nose. "Pumpkins! Crisp red ap-ples! Golden wheat! Mellow peaches! Dear little grapes and big, bold watermelons! It's all part of nature's bounty, people. And

1

that's what we're going to be studying next — Nature's Bounty! A whole month celebrating the wonderful world of the foods we grow — just think of it!"

Okay, I'm thinking of it, Jamie thought sourly. She pushed her curly red hair out of her eyes and glanced around the room. She could see that the rest of her class was thinking of it, too. And most of them didn't look any happier than Jamie felt.

Another problem with Miss Duni was that she loved big, involved class projects. Actually, "loved" wasn't a strong enough word for the way Miss Duni felt about class projects. It would be more accurate to say she *lived* them. And she wanted her classes to *live* them, too.

In fact, that was what she was talking about now. "I don't want anyone in this class holding back when we study Nature's Bounty," Miss Duni said. "It's not enough just to take a bite out of an apple and say you understand how wonderful nature is! No, you have to make yourself a part of the apple's *world*. You have to be planted when it's planted. You have to grow as it grows. You have to fall off the tree with it and feel the way it feels as it's crushed into cider — sad, but also a little bit proud, because you're giving mankind a drink. You have to — "

I know what's coming, thought Jamie.

"You have to *live* the apple's life. Or the grape's life, of course, if you're studying grapes. There's a whole world of wonderful crops out there, people, and we're going to discover *all* of them this month."

Jamie looked over at her best friend, Randy Dowell, who sat next to her. "Well, at least this project can't be any worse than Ancient Egypt was last month," she whispered.

Randy wouldn't look back at her. "Don't whisper so loudly!" she hissed. "We'll get into trouble!"

"Well, Ancient Egypt wasn't so bad for you — you at least got to be the court harpist," Jamie whispered in a quieter voice. "But being the Pharaoh's servant . . . If Miss Duni makes me be something like that *this* time around, I'm dropping out of school."

"Oh, she would never do something like that twice," Randy whispered back comfortingly. "I'm sure you're safe."

"Do you think anyone is ever *really* safe from Bill the Pill?" Jamie answered. "I mean, he *tortured* me during Ancient Egypt!"

Randy had no answer to that.

When the class had studied Ancient Egypt, Jamie's role was a servant of the

Pharaoh, and the boy who played the Pharaoh was her worst enemy in the world — Bill Baird.

Every class has someone like Bill Baird in it, but Bill was the best example of that kind of person that Jamie had ever seen. Tripping people, scaring little kids on their way home from school, dropping girls' homework into the creek — if Bill had to choose between being obnoxious and breathing, he would decide he didn't like air that much, anyway.

And it always seemed as though the main recipient of his obnoxiousness was Jamie.

To make things even worse, Bill Baird sat right behind Jamie in class. Now, as if he'd sensed that she was thinking about him, he jabbed her sharply on the shoulder with a pen cap. "Hey! Quit yakking and pay attention!" he said.

Jamie rubbed her aching shoulder and frowned. A pen-cap jab usually meant a rubber band would be next.

Miss Duni was speaking again. "Now, for this project we're going to be doing something very exciting," she said. "As you all know, the school's Thanksgiving Assembly is coming up at the end of this month. Now, the Pilgrims couldn't just go to the Stop'n'Shop to buy their Thanksgiving food,

4

could they? They ate what they grew —
vegetables and fruit!"

"And big, fat turkeys. Like you, Keenan,"
Bill Baird whispered. *Snnnnap!* went the
rubber band Jamie had been expecting —
right on her neck.

Of course, Miss Duni didn't notice. "Just
like the Pilgrims, we're going to be learning
all about crops and harvesting," she continued. "And we're going to put on a show
about Nature's Bounty for the Thanksgiving Assembly! Isn't that wonderful?"

For a few horrified seconds, the room was
silent. "Yes, Miss Duni," someone finally
said in a weak voice.

"We'll have lots and lots of skits about
where we get our food," Miss Duni went on.
"You'll write them, of course — I want you
all to unleash your creativity. I'll write a
few songs for you, though. I think it's always good to get a little practice singing
solos in front of an audience."

Jamie twisted her fingers together.
Please, please don't write a song for me, she
prayed. If I have to sing a solo in front of
my parents, I'll — A bobbing motion on the
other side of the room caught Jamie's eye.
It was Larry Berman, the biggest hand-
raiser in the class. He'd once raised his
hand 117 times in a single morning —

Jamie had counted.

"Miss Duni, my favorite vegetable is fried eggplant!" said Larry eagerly. "Can I do a skit about eggplant?"

Miss Duni smiled at him. "Sounds good. I don't know if the Pilgrims had eggplant, but they surely would have loved it if they had," she said. "We're going to be working in teams for Nature's Bounty. I thought you might like working with Leesa Alexander."

Jamie glanced over at Randy again, and this time Randy couldn't help grinning back at her. Leesa and Larry were the perfect pair. Leesa was even more of a teacher's pet than Larry was.

"I'd love to work with Larry!" Leesa chirped. "Eggplant's a big favorite of mine. And I like brussels sprouts, too!"

"Perhaps you can write a little skit where brussels sprouts and eggplant have some kind of argument and then become Thanksgiving friends," Miss Duni said. "Now, we need people to do a skit about corn. Who in this class likes corn?"

Every hand in the room stayed where it was except for Larry's. He started to raise his again, then suddenly remembered that he already had a part in the show.

"No one wants to do corn?" Miss Duni sounded disappointed. "Okay, I guess I'll just have to pick someone. You, Starr. You can do the corn skit."

Starr Stuart was the prettiest, snobbiest girl in the class. At Miss Duni's words she smiled proudly, tossed back her blond hair, and said, "How perfect. My hair is the same color as corn silk."

"It certainly is," said Miss Duni. "Now, I'd like Mike Liu and Peter Elliot to be in charge of garlic. Both you boys have nice voices, and I think the garlic skit should have a song or two."

"But there wasn't any garlic at the first Thanksgiving!" protested Mike Liu.

"Oh, that doesn't matter," Miss Duni assured him. "We're thankful for garlic *today*, and that's what counts."

Mike and Peter exchanged horrified glances, but they didn't say anything. It was clear that their teacher had already decided exactly what the Nature's Bounty show was going to be like.

As Miss Duni continued making assignments, Jamie's mind drifted off. She was wondering what she'd do later on that afternoon, when she was invisible.

No matter how awful school got, Jamie's special sneakers could make up for it. They had been a birthday present from her Great-Aunt Letitia. They were great-looking —

7

pink high-tops with green fluorescent laces
— and whenever she put them on, she be-
came invisible.

Unfortunately, the invisibility didn't always work right. Sometimes it took a while
before Jamie disappeared, and sometimes
she would reappear before she was ready.
That could get embarrassing. There was
nothing worse than turning up under the
nose of someone you were spying on. But for
the most part, being able to disappear whenever she wanted to was great.

Maybe I'll put on my sneakers and head
over to the high school to watch Betsy's
cheerleader tryouts, Jamie thought. (Betsy
was one of Jamie's two older sisters. She was
sixteen. Margaret was twelve, and Jamie's
little brother Tim was five.) She said she'd
kill me if she saw me there, but if she *can't*
see me —

"And Jamie, I was wondering if you'd like
to work with Randy," Miss Duni was saying.

Jamie sat upright with a jerk. Work with
Randy! Miss Duni almost never let best
friends work together! "That would be
great, Miss Duni," Jamie said. She and
Randy smiled excitedly at each other.

"Fine. The two of you will do the maple
syrup skit," Miss Duni said.

Jamie stared blankly at her teacher. "Is —

8

is maple syrup a crop?" she asked.

"It certainly is!" said Miss Duni.

"But don't they get maple syrup in the spring?" asked Randy.

"Yes, but that doesn't matter. Nature's Bounty is harvested all year long. Anyway, you mustn't worry about all these little details." Miss Duni's eyes were dreamy. "Think of it, girls. A tree's most valuable possession — its sap. Rows and rows of sugar maples waiting to be tapped so that we can have better breakfasts. It's almost like giving blood, isn't it?"

Jamie and Randy both shuddered. "Kind of," Randy said politely. "Should we be trees in the skit, Miss Duni?"

"Well, maybe the farmer can help you decide," Miss Duni answered.

"The farmer?" Jamie asked. Did Miss Duni assign someone the role of farmer when I wasn't paying attention? she wondered.

"Oh! Didn't I mention that?" said Miss Duni. "The farmer will have a *very* important part in our Nature's Bounty show. Luckily, he's had lots of practice running things."

Suddenly Jamie's stomach lurched. Once again, she knew what was coming. "Oh, no," she breathed.

"I'm talking about our Pharaoh, of course," said Miss Duni. "Bill Baird." She smiled at him. "You did such a good job as Pharaoh that I think you'd be *just* the right person for our class farmer. How does that strike you?"

"I can't wait," said Bill. "I *especially* can't wait to grind up those maple trees into syrup." He kicked the back of Jamie's chair.

Miss Duni laughed indulgently. "Oh, Bill! You know maple trees aren't ground up. All you have to do is tap them — you know, puncture the bark a little."

"Well, I'll look forward to that," said Bill. He gave an evil little chuckle that only Jamie heard. "I'd like to be the farmer, Miss Duni."

"Now, does everyone in the class have a part? I haven't left anyone out, have I?" asked Miss Duni. All around the room, people shook their heads glumly. "Good. Then let's start talking about costumes. First of all, we'll need a *lot* of papier-mâché — "

A loud, crackling sound interrupted her. It was coming from the intercom on the wall next to the flag.

"ATTENTION! ATTENTION! PLEASE HOLD FOR AN IMPORTANT ANNOUNCE-MENT!"

Chapter Two

"Oh, why did they install that intercom?" Miss Duni said irritably. "It's always interrupting!"

There was a gunfire burst of static from the intercom, and the sound of a kid laughing. "*I'll* read it, *I'll* read it!" Jamie heard someone say. "No way!" someone else answered. "It's *my* turn!"

The sound of a throat being cleared blasted into Miss Duni's room. "ATTENTION! ATT — Oops, I already said that," came the voice over the intercom. "There will be a very important meeting after school for all Laughing Eggs — I mean, *Laughing Egg Elementary* students who are interested in helping to start up a school newspaper. The meeting will be held in the auditorium. I can't believe it! I blew it!"

There was a burst of giggles and some static, and then the intercom went dead.

A school paper! Jamie thought. Hey, that sounds great! I've always wanted to be a reporter!

I'll uncover all kinds of scandals, she thought excitedly. Everyone will wonder who my sources are. I'll always be the first on the spot when trouble strikes, and I'll get amazing quotes. No one will believe that a fourth-grader . . .

But Miss Duni wasn't quite as excited as Jamie. "A newspaper!" she snorted. "Ideas for a *newspaper*? You'd think they'd wait until after the Thanksgiving Assembly — we have so little time to prepare. This school's priorities are all wrong!" Miss Duni shook her head. "Well, back to the subject that *really* matters — the Nature's Bounty Show. Who'd like to volunteer their father to make a giant wheelbarrow for the stage? It should be about fifty feet long, with — "

Once again Jamie stopped listening. She couldn't help thinking about the newspaper. And when lunchtime came, she discovered that Randy was also interested.

"Jamie, I've got a really great idea for that newspaper!" Randy burst out as soon as they sat down with their trays. "It would be called 'The History of Laughing Egg'."

Randy stopped to take a bite of sandwich. "See, we'd get these notebooks and go all around town and talk to the people who've lived here for a long time — like Mrs. Wiggins down the street from me — and find out what the town used to be like. Isn't that fantastic? We'd sort of be historians!"

"What kinds of questions would we ask?" Jamie said doubtfully.

"Oh, stuff like when Laughing Egg got its first sidewalks and whether the firehouse has always stood in the same place. Things like that." Randy's wide blue eyes were alight with excitement. "You know — the kinds of questions that people don't usually think of! It would be great, Jamie! I bet we could uncover some really amazing stuff!"

Probably more like some really *boring* stuff, Jamie thought. But since Randy was her best friend, Jamie didn't say that aloud. Instead, she said, "Well, it sounds really — uh — educational, Ran. But I was kind of thinking of something else we could do. Something that might be a little more exciting."

"What could be more fascinating than the history of our town?" Randy asked wonderingly.

"Well, I was thinking of a gossip column," said Jamie. "School gossip, I mean. Who

13

likes who, what the teachers really think of us — you know."

"But Jamie, we'd get into trouble!" said Randy. "People would get mad at us if we wrote gossip about them!"

"No, they wouldn't, Ran. We'd write it anonymously! People would love a column like that. I bet everyone would turn to it first. It would be like something on TV — all the dirt on people's secret lives!"

"Glad to hear you're talking about dirt, Keenan," came a loud voice behind Jamie. "Because you're going to see a lot of it over the next couple of weeks, with all these crops I'm growing."

Jamie didn't have to turn around to know who it was. "Mind your own business, Bill," she said wearily.

"That's *Farmer Baird* to you," said Bill. "I'm a very important person. Everyone depends on the farmer — Miss Duni said so." Suddenly he reached over Jamie's shoulder and grabbed the bag of cookies off her tray. "Hey, chocolate chip! My favorite!" He popped one of them into his mouth. "Ugh!" he said with his mouth full. Crumbs sprayed all over the table. "Your mother makes terrible cookies!"

"My *father* made those!" said Jamie. "Give them back!" She half-rose in her seat

14

and tried to grab the bag out of Bill's hand.

"Come on, Bill!" Randy begged. "Give them to her!"

"Take it easy!" Bill said. "I'll give them back in a minute."

He dropped the bag of cookies on the floor. As Jamie reached for it, he ground it into dust with his heel.

"Oops! Sorry," he said. "You don't need that sweet stuff, anyway. Not with all the maple syrup I'm going to be squeezing out of you."

With that, he swaggered away.

"Well, Ran," said Jamie after a second, "I can see the headlines now. FOURTH-GRADE STUDENT MURDERED BY CLASSMATE. 'HE JUST DROVE ME CRAZY,' SHE SAYS. That would make an excellent article for the new paper. Anyway, I'm going to that meeting after school. Do you want to come?"

"Of course," said Randy. "I just know the editors will love my idea."

"Come in and sit down, everybody!" someone yelled from the auditorium's stage. School had just let out, and the newspaper meeting was about to begin.

"Oh, let's not work on the paper after all, Jamie," said Randy nervously. "There are

15

mostly fifth and sixth-graders here."

Jamie peered in through the auditorium door. Randy was right. Jamie hardly knew any of the kids who were sitting in the seats.

"It's okay, Randy," she said, trying to reassure herself as much as her friend. "We can sit in the back."

"No, let's forget about it. You know, I'm really not as interested in working on a newspaper as I thought — "

"Come *on*, Randy," Jamie interrupted. "What are they going to do, kill us?" She grabbed Randy's arm and propelled her through the door.

"Sit down! Sit down, everybody!" called a black-haired girl who was sitting on the stage. Jamie did recognize *her*. Her name was Cass O'Brian, and she was the president of the Student Council. "Let's get organized here! We've got a lot of business to attend to!" Cass shouted.

Gradually most of the noise in the auditorium died down, and Cass stood up. "Thank you," she said. She glanced down at a clipboard she was holding. "Now, as you know, we'd like to start a newspaper at Laughing Egg Elementary. It's really terrible how none of the students have any voice in this school — "

"What are you going to call the paper?"

16

someone shouted.

"We'll be taking suggestions about that later," said Cass. "Our first order of business now is to — "

"Why don't you call it 'The Doo Doo Delight'?" someone else shouted.

Cass cleared her throat. "You don't *have* to be here, people," she said.

I bet she'll be a teacher when she grows up, Jamie thought. Cass says "people" just like Miss Duni.

"If you want," Cass continued, "the other editors and I can just have a closed meeting. We don't need any help from — "

"Call it 'The Toilet Times'!" yelled a third kid. There were sputters of laughter from all over the auditorium.

"I'm just going to ignore those few people who want to ruin things for the majority," said Cass. "If you don't *want* to be mature, that's your problem."

Silence descended on the room. "Now," she went on, "the first thing we need to do is to come up with some good ideas for articles for the first issue. The principal is giving us our own office, and we can use the school copying machines. So if we can think of some ideas, we can get the first issue out pretty fast!"

"How about putting all the teachers in

jail?" someone called.

Finally, it was decided that the paper would be called "The Laughing Egg Times"; Cass would be the editor-in-chief; and the fifth and sixth-graders would write all the good articles. Then everyone stood up and started putting on their coats.

"I told you we shouldn't have come!" Randy muttered. "They don't want little kids around!"

"We're not little kids," said Jamie stoutly. She jumped to her feet and pulled Randy up next to her. "Cass," she called, "we have some ideas for the paper, too."

"Yo! Fourthies want to talk!" hooted a boy in front of Jamie and Randy. "Let's get out of here!"

"Quiet down, everyone!" yelled Cass. "We need to give *everyone* a chance, even if they're too young to understand what we've been talking about! What are your ideas, kids?" she asked.

I don't think I've ever seen so many eyes staring at me, Jamie thought nervously. "Uh — uh — Randy has a very good idea, anyway," Jamie said in a wobbly voice. She elbowed Randy in the ribs.

"What's your idea, Randy?" called Cass. "C'mon, hurry up! The buses are waiting!"

Randy opened and closed her mouth a few

times. "A — a history of the town," she said finally.

"BORING! BORING!" shouted the boy in front of them.

"Shut up, Steve!" said Cass sternly. She smiled at Randy. "That's a good idea, but it's not quite right for our paper. Maybe when you're in fifth or sixth grade, you'll be able to come up with something more interesting. Okay, everyone, meeting is adjourned."

"All right! We're out of here!" shouted Steve.

Everyone began rushing toward the door. Only Jamie and Randy stayed where they were. Jamie turned to look at Randy. Her friend was staring at the ground, her face red and her chin quivering. Jamie knew she felt terrible.

Hey, wait a minute! Jamie thought. We're not going to let the big kids treat us like babies! This newspaper is supposed to be for the whole school! She pulled Randy up to the front of the stage. Cass was just putting her books into her knapsack. "Cass, could we talk to you for a second?" Jamie asked. "I've got an idea, too."

Cass sighed. "Okay, but make it quick."

Jamie darted a glance around the auditorium to make sure no one else could hear her.

"How about a gossip column?" she said in a low voice. "We could write an anonymous gossip column! You could call it 'The Talking Egg'! We'd get all kinds of gossip, and no one would know who The Talking Egg was!"

"Jamie, I told you I don't *want* to write a— " Randy began. But Cass cut her off.

"A gossip column," she said in a thoughtful voice. "You know, we *should* have something like that. And 'The Talking Egg' is a great name. Thanks, Jamie! A gossip column would be perfect! I don't think kids your age are up to writing something like that, though. I'd better get someone else to write it."

"I think you're right. We're definitely not — " Randy began.

Jamie stepped hard on Randy's foot. "We can do it," she said. "We'll have a column on your desk the day after tomorrow."

"I'll look forward to it," Cass said. She jumped off the stage and headed for the door.

Randy was staring at Jamie as if she'd gone crazy. "Jamie, what are you *talking* about?" she sputtered. "How are we going to get enough gossip to write a column in one day? How are we going to get *any* gossip at all?"

There was a broad smile on Jamie's face. "How else, Ran? The pink sneakers!"

Chapter Three

"But Jamie, using the magic sneakers still seems illegal to me!" Randy protested half an hour later. "I mean, it's *unfair* to sneak around and spy on people and then write about them! Wouldn't it be nicer just to ask people to tell us some gossip?"

"Of course it would, if they *would* tell us some — but they wouldn't!" answered Jamie. "Come on, Randy. Can you really see us going up to some sixth-grade girl and saying, 'Is it true that you're in love with Mr. Bissell?' She'd either laugh in our faces or kill us!"

It was four o'clock in the afternoon, and Jamie and Randy had just gotten back to Randy's house. They were in the kitchen now, frying up a batch of homemade dough-nut holes. Jamie was rolling the dough and

21

dropping it into the fry kettle, and Randy was fishing out the finished doughnut holes and covering them with powdered sugar. The entire kitchen was covered with drifts of powdered sugar and blobs of oil. Randy's mother was upstairs, and Jamie hoped she wouldn't come down before they had a chance to clean up.

For the last hour Jamie had been trying to convince Randy that the "Talking Egg" column would be a great idea. But she was getting nowhere.

Basically, Randy's worries all boiled down to the same two things. She was worried about being mean to other people, and she was worried about getting into trouble.

"Look, Ran," Jamie said at last. "How about if I gather all the gossip myself? And if you're worried about our being too mean — well, you can write the column and you could write it any way you wanted!"

Randy thought about that for a moment. "Maybe that would be okay," she said at last. "Sure! That would be fun. But I don't have to sign my name, do I?"

"No. Definitely not. You're The Talking Egg, that's all."

Randy smiled, and Jamie could tell she liked the idea of a secret name. "The Talking Egg," Randy repeated. "Talking Egg

Dowell. It sounds good. But where can we — you, I mean — get some gossip? Are you just going to turn invisible and walk around the halls?"

Jamie grinned. "Nope. I was thinking about this on the way home. And I decided that the teachers' lounge would be the best place to start."

"The teachers' lounge!" Randy gasped. "But Jamie, what if you suddenly turn visible again in front of all those teachers? You'll get into a *lot* of — "

"No, I won't get into trouble," Jamie said firmly. "Now you'd better check those doughnut holes again, Ran. We want them brown, not black."

Randy peered into the pot of bubbling oil. "Maybe you can bring a bag of these to the teachers in the lounge," she suggested.

"Nice thought, Ran, but I think the teachers might have a little trouble with an invisible doughnut delivery-person. I think we can eat them all ourselves."

"Jamie, can I ask you something?" asked Jamie's twelve-year-old sister Margaret when Jamie sat down at the breakfast table the next morning. "Why are you wearing one pair of sneakers and carrying another?"

Jamie shoved the pink high-tops under

24

the table as she sat down. "Gym today," she said quickly.

"But you have gym every day at your school!" put in Jamie's sister Betsy. "You've been complaining about it since school started!"

"That's not fair! I haven't complained in weeks! I'm pretty good at gym now!" Jamie protested.

"I'll believe it when I see it," said Betsy, pushing around the raw cabbage on her plate with her fork. Betsy was always on a diet. Her latest nutrition theory was that she'd lose weight if she ate only uncooked, green vegetables.

"I bet she really brings another pair of sneakers to change into when Billy Baird's around," said Margaret. "He likes girls who wear pink, you know."

"Margaret, shut up!" shouted Jamie at the top of her lungs.

Mr. Keenan flinched and put down the newspaper. "Jamie, was that necessary?" he asked.

"Yes, Dad! It was! Margaret's always trying to marry me off to that slime-weasel!"

"Honey, please don't talk like that at the breakfast table," said Mrs. Keenan. "Save it for the playground."

"Jamie's only trying to disguise her true

feelings," said Margaret, and she and Betsy both grinned.

"What is a snime-weasel?" asked Jamie's little brother Tim. He pushed a toy truck through his plate of scrambled eggs.

"*Slime*-weasel, Tim," she corrected him. "A slime-weasel is a gross, horrible, disgusting person like Bill Baird. And Margaret," she added.

Tim looked up with interest. "Can he come over and play with me?"

"Sure!" said Betsy instantly. "Jamie, why don't you ask him to come over after school? You can model your pink sneakers for him. Why *are* you bringing them to school, anyway?"

I can't take any more of this, Jamie thought. Hastily she scooped up the sneakers from under the table and rushed for the front door. "Gotta go, Mom," she yelled back over her shoulder. "I think I hear the bus."

Mrs. Keenan half-rose in her chair. "Jamie, the bus won't be here for another fifteen minutes!" she said.

"Can't hear you! I'm already out the door! Bye!" Jamie called over her shoulder.

Miss Duni had another one of her surprises waiting for the class that morning. She had pushed all the desks into one corner

26

of the classroom, fenced it off, and covered the floor with dirt. She had also covered her entire desk with burlap.

Miss Duni hadn't neglected her own appearance, either. She was sitting right on the desk, dressed from head to toe in Pilgrim clothes. She even had on big, clunky shoes with iron buckles!

"Good morning, people," she said cheerfully. "Welcome to Plymouth Rock — that's what my desk represents — and welcome to the fields of the Pilgrims!"

Already, Jamie saw, the dirt from the "fields" had done a pretty good job of migrating across the rest of the classroom floor. As everyone in the class began tiptoeing gingerly toward their desks, Jamie was glad she was wearing jeans. Starr Stuart — who was wearing a leather miniskirt, a white cashmere sweater, white stockings, and short white boots — was having a lot of trouble.

"I guess you'll all have to start wearing workboots to school!" chirped Miss Duni in her normal voice. She jumped up from her desk. "Now we can actually plant the crops we're studying!"

"It's great! Wherever did you get all the dirt, Miss Duni?" said Leesa Alexander.

"Oh, I rented a pickup truck and drove

around the countryside with a shovel. Wherever I saw a nice patch of dirt, I just scooped it up and tossed it in! Some of the people I borrowed it from were kind of obnoxious about it." Miss Duni sounded puzzled. "I don't know why. I *told* them I'd return it when we were done with the Thanksgiving Assembly. After all, isn't it more important to give a group of students the chance to learn about where we get our food than to worry about some old farm?"

"Anyway," Miss Duni continued, "this morning we're going to divide into our groups and begin planning our skits for the show. I'm giving all the groups half an hour to talk together while I start composing some songs. Then we'll all hear your ideas. Now, where's our farmer?"

Jamie heard a scraping noise behind her as Bill Baird pushed his chair back across the gritty floor. "Here I am," he said.

"And who's working with you?" asked Miss Duni. "Oh, yes — Jamie and Randy. Okay, you three. In half an hour, I want to hear your most glorious ideas for a skit about how maple syrup is produced. Now have a great time!"

As Miss Duni began organizing the rest of the groups, Jamie slowly turned her chair so that she was facing Bill. Randy did the same.

28

With a smirk, Bill put his feet up on his desk and leaned back. "Okay, you two," he said. "Start writing that skit."

"Sorry, Bill!" Jamie answered breezily. "We're fresh out of ideas!"

"What do you mean?" Bill demanded, scowling. "Get going! We've only got half an hour!"

Jamie gave him a regretful smile. "I'm afraid we just can't come up with anything," she said. "We're so thrilled to be working with you that it's hard to think."

Unfortunately, Randy didn't join in. Instead she cast a scared glance over at Miss Duni, who was humming and thumping her desk as she composed her song.

"Miss Duni will want to hear *something*," Randy said nervously. "I was sort of thinking about this last night, and I thought we could maybe look up maple syrup in the encyclopedia. It might give us some ideas."

"Well, what are you waiting for? Go get the encyclopedia!" Bill ordered.

"I have it right here," Randy said, reaching down next to her desk. Quickly she thumbed through the pages. "Here we go. Look, they even have a picture!"

She held out the book to Jamie and Bill. Next to the entry called Maple Syrup was a picture of a farmer dressed in old-fashioned clothes. He was cracking his whip over the heads of two huge oxen, who were straining to pull a wagon loaded with vats of sap toward a fire.

"Hey, that's me! That's who I am!" shouted Bill, pointing at the farmer. "And you guys can be the oxen! Miss Duni, we're ready to tell you our idea for our skit!" he called out.

"Sorry, Bill, we're not going to be oxen," said Jamie scornfully. "Maybe we could be — uh, girls from the farm next door. You could have asked us to help you, or — "

"Or maybe I could be your wife or something, and Jamie could be our daughter," put in Randy.

Yuck! thought Jamie. How can she *think* of being his wife — even in a play?

Randy was looking really excited now. "Say we're a poor, struggling farm family, and our only hope is this one maple tree. All our other trees have died. Only this one is still alive. We could tend it so carefully that—"

"Maybe we even try some old Indian remedies to keep it healthy," added Jamie.

"And it gives so much sap that the farm is saved!" finished Randy triumphantly.

But Bill wasn't listening. He was still trying to get Miss Duni's attention, and she

30

was having some kind of discussion about Starr Stuart's hair with Starr and Judy Gollin. "But corn silk is supposed to be wavy!" Starr was saying. "I *must* get a perm for the show!"

At last Miss Duni came over to Bill's desk. "What is it, dear?" she asked.

"Miss Duni, look at this!" said Bill. He pointed to the picture. "See, I'm the farmer, and Randy and Jamie can be the oxen. Isn't that great?"

"Oh, what an original idea!" gasped Miss Duni before Jamie or Randy could say anything. "I just can't wait to see what kind of skit you'll write. Good work, kids!"

Then she drifted off down the aisle.

"You know, maybe being oxen wouldn't really be so bad," said Randy after a second. "The wagon could be really, really heavy, and we're struggling to pull it . . ."

To Jamie's dismay, Randy was getting all starry-eyed. "And we collapse and fall to our knees . . ."

"And I yank you to your feet with my incredible muscle power, and the crop is saved!" said Bill.

Randy smiled happily at him. "And everyone bursts into applause," she said.

Jamie was so angry she could hardly talk. "That's the most terrible idea I've ever heard," she choked out. "It's so — so cruel to animals! And to us!" She didn't care about the shocked, hurt look on Randy's face. How could Randy even consider being in such a humiliating skit? "I wouldn't dress up as an ox if you paid me," Jamie said. "I'm not crawling around on any stage with a yoke around my neck. Not *ever.*"

"Well, that's too bad," Bill drawled. "Because Randy and I both think it's a good idea. So that makes it two against one. And then there's Miss Duni, so it's really three against one."

My own best friend has betrayed me, thought Jamie bitterly. She wants me to be the ox of my worst enemy.

There just *had* to be some way of getting out of this skit!

Maybe I can get my mom to tell Miss Duni it's against our family's religion to imitate animals, Jamie thought.

Maybe I can figure out a way to rent some *real* oxen for the skit instead, and convince Miss Duni that they're really us in incredibly lifelike costumes.

Or maybe I can just sneak out to my locker, put on my magic sneakers, and disappear from the face of the earth.

Chapter Four

"Oh, that's all right, Ran," Jamie said kindly. "I know you didn't really mean to agree with Bill the Pill's terrible idea for the Nature's Bounty show. We'll think of something better together and tell Miss Duni we've changed our minds." Jamie gave Randy a smile of true forgiveness.

Unfortunately, Randy didn't see it — Jamie was talking to her own reflection in the girls' bathroom after school. Randy had already gone home.

It's so weird to think of Randy going along with *anything* Bill Baird would suggest! thought Jamie. I wonder if she . . . But Jamie shook that thought off. There was no way Randy could have a crush on Bill. She was probably just excited about doing something Miss Duni liked so much.

Well, I'll convince Randy later, Jamie told herself. Now it's time to go gossip-gathering.

Jamie laced up the pink high-tops and sat down on a bench, waiting to turn invisible. This time it took about five minutes before she disappeared. She stowed her regular sneakers under the bench and walked quietly into the hall.

The teachers' lounge was on the third floor. Just as Jamie reached the door, she heard a brassy voice inside the lounge blaring, "Okay, Wendy. I'll call his parents for you. I don't know how they can let their own kid get away with that kind of stuff!"

Footsteps thundered toward the door, and Jamie leaped hastily out of the way as it swung open. Out strode Mrs. Lapham, whom everyone knew as the loudest teacher in the school. As Mrs. Lapham began to close the door behind her, Jamie ducked under her arm into the lounge.

There. She was inside. But to Jamie's disappointment, the teachers' lounge didn't look like a very exciting place.

I thought it would be a lot fancier in here, she thought. A TV, a stereo, some big, cozy chairs, maybe a couple of computers and a candy machine — not a bunch of wrecked-up plastic chairs and a rickety old table!

Three teachers were sitting at the table correcting papers. One was Mrs. Franklin. She taught third grade and directed the school play every fall. The second woman at the table was a fifth-grade teacher named Mrs. DiNapoli. Across from them sat Mr. Bissell, the sixth-grade teacher who was the heartthrob of practically every sixth-grade girl.

As Jamie watched, Mrs. DiNapoli put down her red pen and rubbed her eyes.

"Tough day?" said Mrs. Franklin.

Mrs. DiNapoli nodded wearily. "My kids just sat like lumps and stared at me. I swear, sometimes I think I'm teaching boiled potatoes instead of fifth-graders!"

A *teacher* is talking like this? thought Jamie in astonishment.

"It's funny," Mrs. Franklin mused, "but I never seem to have that problem. My students all just *love* me, and I love them all — equally. Each and every one of my kids is just as dear to me as if they were my own children."

"Interesting," said Mrs. DiNapoli dryly, "considering that you don't have any children of your own." She changed the subject. "Have you chosen the school play yet?"

"Well, we're not announcing it until next month, but it's going to be 'Mary Poppins,'"

Mrs. Franklin told her.

"Oh, gross!" Jamie groaned aloud.

Mrs. Franklin looked startled. "What's gross about it?" she demanded. "It's an adorable story!"

"I didn't say anything," said Mrs. Di-Napoli. "I agree with you — it *is* a cute story! Who do you think will be Mary Poppins?"

Mrs. Franklin sighed. "Well, I know one little girl who will expect to be chosen — Starr Stuart. Of course, I love all children *equally*, but Starr can sometimes be just a little difficult. She told me this week that she expected to be the lead no matter what play we decide to do. She said she's too talented to be overlooked, even if she's just a fourth-grader."

"That child is everywhere," said Mrs. Di-Napoli crossly. "If I see her in one more TV ad, I'm going to throw up. *Talented*! The only talent she has is for sniffing out a camera and sticking her face in front of it!"

Mrs. Franklin looked a little shocked. Before she could answer, though, Mr. Bissell spoke up. "I've heard a lot about Starr," he said, "and I have to tell you — I pray that she won't wind up in my sixth-grade class."

Both women laughed sympathetically. "The girls after you again?" asked Mrs. Di-Napoli.

Mr. Bissell sighed. "Are they ever! I found a love note on my desk this morning from Leslie Rudman." Jamie pricked up her ears. It would be no problem remembering Starr's name for the column, but she didn't know Leslie. She repeated the name to herself several times to make sure she wouldn't forget it.

At that moment the door opened again, and Mr. Norquist, the school's gym teacher, came in. He walked over to a chair and collapsed into it.

"We are going to lose every football game this season," he said with a groan. "Then we're going to lose every basketball game. Also every volleyball game, every baseball game, and every relay race. Plus soccer, plus — "

"I guess you just finished football practice. Am I right?" asked Mr. Bissell.

"If you can call it football," said Mr. Norquist with a groan. "I'd call it falling-in-the-mud practice, with a little banging-helmets-together practice thrown in. Not that banging their helmets together will hurt these kids. They don't have any brains in there anyway."

Suddenly Mr. Norquist sat up. "What's *that*?" he asked. "Look! A hand is floating on the wall!"

He was pointing right at Jamie.

Jamie glanced down at herself — and realized with a shudder of horror that he was right. One of her hands was visible. How can I be reappearing so quickly? she wondered. This has never happened before!

Quickly she ducked down behind one of the plastic chairs.

"I don't see anything," said Mrs. DiNapoli.

"It's gone now," said Mr. Norquist. "But it was definitely there. A child's hand, just floating in the air." He shivered. "I wonder . . . do you think a murder was committed in here long ago or something?"

The three other teachers were staring at him as though he'd suddenly grown wings. "A *murder*?" asked Mrs. DiNapoli. "In the teachers' lounge?"

"Well, why else would there be a floating hand in here?" asked Mr. Norquist.

"But there *isn't* a floating hand in here, Fred," said Mrs. Franklin gently.

"I know there isn't one *now*!" Mr. Norquist snapped. "It vanished — just like the soul of the poor murdered child it used to belong to."

The three other teachers were staring at Mr. Norquist in alarm. "Fred," asked Mr. Bissell, "did anything weird happen to you

38

during football practice? Did the football hit you on the head or anything?"

Jamie couldn't help giggling. And this time all four teachers looked in her direction.

"A ghostly laugh!" yelled Mr. Norquist. "Didn't you hear it? Spirit, why have you come to torture us?"

"I did hear it," said Mrs. DiNapoli grimly. "You're right, Fred. Someone's in here. It's no murdered child, though. Someone's hiding in this room." She stood up and walked over toward Jamie.

Oh, no, Jamie thought in a panic. I'm going to reappear any second!

Quickly she looked around for a way out. She spotted an unopened cup of strawberry yogurt sitting on a nearby chair. Just before Mrs. DiNapoli reached the spot where Jamie was hiding, Jamie stood up and flung the yogurt as hard as she could against the window.

It hit the glass with a splat. A pink puddle of yogurt began to drip down the pane, and after a minute the empty yogurt container skittered to the ground.

"Hey! Some kids on the playground are throwing stuff at us!" shouted Mr. Bissell.

All four teachers whipped around to see what had happened — and Jamie dashed for the door. The minute she was out in the hall, she reappeared.

That was *too* close, she told herself, panting as she raced down the hall. But I sure have some great stuff to tell Randy!

"And then Mr. Norquist said none of the football players had any brains anyway!" Jamie finished triumphantly. She'd changed out of her pink sneakers and headed straight for Randy's house. "Pretty good quotes for my first day on the job, don't you think? Listen, Ran, do you think you can write a column right now? Because then I can drop it off at the newspaper office on my way home."

"Sure," said Randy. She took out a pink notepad with pictures of kittens on it and sat down in a businesslike way at her desk. "Just make yourself at home."

For the next half hour Randy was bent over her desk while Jamie walked restlessly around her room trying not to peek over Randy's shoulder. At last Randy tore out the sheet of paper, folded it, and handed it to Jamie, who began to unfold it.

"NO, NO!" Randy shrieked. "DON'T READ IT IN FRONT OF ME! It's too embarrassing!"

Jamie laughed. "Okay, Randy. I won't. I

think we're a great team, though. Thanks a lot! Tomorrow we'll decide who to write about next!"

Jamie was almost skipping as she left Randy's house. She hadn't gotten caught. They were turning the story in even before they said they would. Cass wouldn't believe how professional they were, and what good, rich gossip they'd managed to dig up . . .

Jamie waited until she was out of sight of Randy's house before she unfolded the sheet of paper and began to read Randy's neat, round writing.

"Oh, no," she whispered.

This is what Randy had written:

AN INTERESTING AFTERNOON
by The Talking Egg

We all know that teachers need a place to relax, and that's what the lounge is for. Today the lounge was a place of many different and interesting conversations. Mrs. Franklin discussed who will be in the cast of the new play she will be putting on, called "Mary Poppins." "Mary Poppins" is the wonderful story of a magical nanny who brings all kinds of adventures to the Banks household!

Another topic of discussion was this fall's football team. Mr. Norquist hopes they will do a good job. Mr. Bissell and Mrs. DiNapoli talked about some of their students. All in all, a very interesting afternoon was had by all.

"This isn't gossip," Jamie groaned. "This is just Randy trying not to say anything mean!"

Jamie pulled a pen out of her jeans pocket and sat down on the curb. "I've got to fix this," she muttered, "or Cass will laugh us out of school."

It took only a few minutes. When Jamie was done, the pink sheet of paper was a mess from all the crossouts she'd made — but she knew Cass would like it. She stuck the pen back into her pocket and raced toward school to drop off the column.

It wasn't until Jamie got home that she remembered that she and Randy hadn't had a chance to talk about changing the oxen skit.

Oh, well, we can figure that out tomorrow, she decided. Randy will be so glad I fixed her article that she'll probably be happy to do me a favor.

Jamie smiled proudly. Where would this reporting team be without me? she thought. Just think — tomorrow the paper will come out, and we'll be famous!

Chapter Five

Jamie raced through the front door and ran down the corridor the next morning. She was so eager to see how the newspaper looked that she'd gotten to school an hour early. Even so, Cass O'Brian was already there — waiting by Jamie's locker. In her hands was a big stack of newspapers.

"Hi, Cass!" Jamie panted. "Let me see a paper!"

"We finished stapling the pages together this morning, so I'm going to pass them out before school starts," said Cass. "I wanted to give you your copy right away. You really did a great job, Jamie. Wherever did you get all this juicy stuff?"

"Oh, I have my ways," Jamie told her with what she hoped was a cool little smile. Actually, she wanted to throw her books

44

into the air and scream with pride, but she didn't think a sixth-grader would appreciate that.

"Well, keep up the good work," Cass said. "And tell Randy I said congratulations."

But when Randy read the paper herself a few minutes later, she didn't seem to think congratulations were in order.

"Jamie," she said accusingly, "this isn't what I wrote." She held out her copy of The Laughing Egg Times. And she pointed to a page that Jamie had — by then — read about twenty times.

THE TALKING EGG

Get ready to barf, fans — the next school play is "Mary Poppins." Mrs. Franklin, the play's director, is not too happy about the girl who wants to star in the play — Starr Stuart, that is. The blond fourth-grader is trying to push her way into the lead AGAIN . . . . And speaking of pushy, Leslie Rudman's latest love letter to Mr. Bissell was *not* appreciated. Please believe the Talking Egg, girls — Mr. Bissell ISN'T interested. Not now, not ever . . . . A certain fifth-grade teacher compared her class to

45

boiled potatoes when she thought she was safe in the teachers' lounge — but that's nothing compared to what Mr. Norquist thinks of the football team. As far as Coach is concerned, guys, your helmets aren't protecting much underneath. Don't take him too seriously, though. He's been seeing things lately. What kinds of things? Tune in next issue, and The Talking Egg just may let you in on the secret.

"You rewrote the whole thing!" Randy whispered.

"Oh, Ran, I did not," Jamie whispered back. "I just made a few changes. It wasn't gossipy enough before. Hey, why are you opening my locker?"

Each girl knew the other's locker combination, and Randy was turning the dial on Jamie's locker now. She yanked open the locker door and pulled out a sweater Jamie had stuffed down at the bottom and forgotten about. "I'm just getting back that sweater you borrowed three weeks ago!" she snapped. "Do you mind? Anyway, the column is *too* gossipy now. Besides, you didn't even ask me if it was okay to 'make a few changes.' You should have checked with me!"

46

"I — I know," Jamie said uncomfortably. "I won't do it again, Ran. I promise."

Then Jamie brightened. "But look — everyone's reading the paper! We're famous!"

It was true. All up and down the hall, heads were bent over the newspaper.

When the bell rang and the girls headed to their classroom, they found that everyone was talking about The Talking Egg.

"Whoever wrote this certainly isn't very respectful to teachers," said Larry Berman angrily.

"Aw, it's all made-up anyway," said Bill Baird.

"It's got to be," said Peter Elliot. He was one of the best athletes in the fourth grade. "Everyone knows the Omelettes are going to have a winning season. We're the greatest!" The Omelettes was the name of Laughing Egg Elementary School's football team.

"What do *you* think of The Talking Egg, Starr?" Jamie called out slyly.

Starr tossed her head. "I haven't read it. But if I had, I'd say it was *incredibly* stupid. Everyone knows I'll get the lead in the play."

All her friends nodded loyally. "Anyway, being in The Talking Egg shows that you're famous in this school," said Judy Gollin. "Of course, I haven't read it either," she added hastily when she saw Starr's face. "I just mean it's kind of a — a compliment that you're in it. That's all."

"I guess you're right," said Starr after a second.

A compliment, Jamie mused. If it's such a compliment, maybe The Talking Egg should pay Starr a *really* big compliment. Maybe we should devote a whole column to her!

Suddenly Miss Duni's voice broke into Jamie's thoughts. The teacher was perched up on Plymouth Rock, tapping her foot impatiently. "People, would you *please* forget about that paper?" she asked. "Let's keep our minds on the important things — like how the plants we're studying get the water they need so desperately. I wrote a song about that just last night."

Half an hour later, Miss Duni was singing yet another song — this time one she'd written about root vegetables.

"With leafy tops so lacy and green . . ." she trilled just as Jamie cautiously slid a folded piece of paper onto Randy's desk.

Hi, Ran, the note said. *How 'bout if I do the next column about Starr Stuart? Like if I follow her around this afternoon, maybe?* In a few minutes, Randy slid her return message back onto Jamie's desk.

Hi!!! Okay, but be careful! Better not send me any more notes — I'm sure Miss Duni is watching. And Jamie, don't get into trouble!!!!!

"Are you ready to do my hair, Polly?" Starr asked.

The woman behind the counter at the Laughing Egg Beauty Nest checked her appointment book. "I certainly am," she said, smiling pleasantly. "And your friend?' asked Polly. "Will she — "

"Oh, Judy's just keeping me company," said Starr. Judy nodded. "Don't pay any attention to her."

School had ended about half an hour ago. Jamie had quickly put on the pink sneakers, which she'd stowed in her locker, and followed Starr and Judy out the door. They had led her to the Laughing Egg Beauty Nest.

"It's not a great-looking place," Starr explained to Judy as they walked up the front steps. "But they give me a break on the price because I'm a model." Starr did a lot of modeling for Laughing Egg clothing stores. "I guess they think I'll bring in more business. You can go here from now on, if you like," she added carelessly.

"Oh, I will, Starr," said Judy. "I definitely will."

49

Judy would walk into the center of the sun if Starr told her to, Jamie thought scornfully. Still invisible, she settled herself against the wall, waiting to hear Starr incriminate herself.

She couldn't believe the first thing out of Starr's mouth.

"Make it a little blonder this time, Polly," Starr ordered. "I'm going to be in a play. I'm playing an important part, and my hair has to look like corn silk."

Polly picked up a white plastic bottle and showed it to Starr. "This is called Light Golden Honey Blond," she said. "How does that sound?"

Starr shrugged. "Fine. As long as it's really light."

She dyes her hair? Jamie marvelled. I always thought it was natural!

Starr glanced sharply at Judy. "Now, remember, you promised not to tell anyone about this!"

"Of *course* I promise," breathed Judy. "I *swear*, Starr."

Starr relaxed again. "Anyway, I really am kind of a natural blond," she said. "At least I was blond when I was a baby. This stuff just highlights my natural color."

"Oh, I'm sure it does," said Judy. She — and Jamie — watched with interest as Polly smeared a gooey cream-colored liquid all over Starr's hair. "It needs to stay on for fifteen minutes," the hairdresser told Starr. "Would you like a magazine or something?"

"No," Starr told her. "I'll just talk to Judy." She leaned back in the chair and closed her eyes. Polly slipped back to her desk and began adding up some receipts with a pocket calculator.

For a few minutes there was silence. Judy just stared at Starr respectfully as Starr sat there breathing.

When Starr finally spoke, she sounded a little sleepy. "Did you see Peter Burbank staring at me during recess?" she asked. Peter Burbank was a fifth-grader.

"Not really," said Judy. "Was he?"

"Of course he was!" Starr snapped. "I think he likes me."

"Oh, I'm sure he does!" Judy said quickly. "You know, come to think of it, I *did* see him looking at you. He's cute, Starr! Do you like him?"

"Well, don't tell anyone this — but I think I do," said Starr. "You know, it's been kind of hard for me to find a boy who was *right* for me — with my career and all. I mean, I can't just like someone ordinary, you know?"

Judy nodded solemnly. "But how are you going to let him know you like him?"

"How?" Starr sounded surprised. "I'll just tell him, of course! He'll be thrilled to hear it!"

She's so conceited, Jamie thought. I wish there were some way I could . . . No, I just can't. I'm a reporter. I can't play tricks on Starr.

"You see," Starr went on, "when you're as good-looking as I am, it's okay to tell boys you like them. It's not being too pushy — it's a compliment, really. That's probably something an ordinary-looking person like you wouldn't understand."

"I guess not," said Judy.

"*Definitely* not. But then, of course, a person like you could *never* get away with just going up to a boy and telling him you like him. You're so — "

Suddenly Starr stopped and opened her eyes. "Why are you fidgeting so much?" she asked suspiciously. "You're not bored, are you?"

"No, of course not!" said Judy. "I just have to go to the bathroom!"

"Well, go, then!" said Starr. "It's over there!" And she pointed Judy in the right direction.

Judy trotted off toward the bathroom, and Starr closed her eyes again. Jamie shot a quick glance at Polly. Polly was still sitting at her desk using the calculator. She seemed to have forgotten all about Starr.

This is my chance, Jamie said to herself. I don't *care* if I'm a reporter. I'm not going to let Starr get away with bragging like that. She's got to learn a lesson!

Jamie tiptoed cautiously over to Starr's chair. On the counter in front of Starr was a row of bottles — more hair dyes.

Jet Black, Jamie read. Mahogany Mocha. Autumn Red. Ice Blue . . .

Well, we can skip Ice Blue, Jamie decided, but the other colors sound like fun . . .

Quickly she picked up the bottle of Jet Black and squeezed a thin trickle of black dye onto Starr's head. Then she held her breath, waiting to see what would happen.

Starr didn't move. Her eyelids didn't even flicker. Her breathing was deep and steady. She'd fallen asleep!

Jamie grabbed the bottles of Autumn Red and Mahogany Mocha and squeezed twin rivulets of dye over Starr's hair in a lovely swirling pattern.

Unfortunately, a little of the dye trickled onto Starr's neck. With a start, she woke up — just as Judy came back from the bathroom. "I thought you were getting your hair dyed blond!" said Judy.

"What are you talking about? Of course I'm — "

Then Starr saw herself in the mirror.

"POLLY!" she screamed.

Polly rushed over and stared at Starr in horror. "What happened to your hair?"

"I don't know!" shouted Starr. "I fell asleep for one second, and when I woke up your stupid dye had changed color! It's all *your* stupid fault! My parents are going to sue you!"

"Honey, I didn't do anything!" said Polly. "You must have fallen over onto the bottles of dye while you were sleeping!"

Starr took a deep breath. "Get this stuff out of my hair," she said through clenched teeth. "I want you to turn me blond again. I want that corn silk back. Right away."

Polly bit her lip. "Honey, I'm afraid you're not going to like what I have to say. The dye was on for too long to get it out. The only way to cover it up is to dye it all black."

As Starr opened her mouth to scream again, Jamie moved quickly toward the door.

I guess *I'll* get out while I'm still invisible, she thought cheerfully. Besides, I have the feeling that I might go deaf if I stick around.

Chapter Six

THE TALKING EGG

Everyone wants to look their best — especially Starr Stuart, Laughing Egg's most glamorous fourth-grader. Yesterday, Starr had a trip to the beauty parlor with her friend, Judy. Even though the results weren't quite as good as Starr expected, we're sure she'll still look very nice.

Jamie looked up from the sheet of paper Randy had just handed her. "Randy, this isn't gossip!" she said in dismay. "It sounds like a book report or something!"

Once again Jamie and Randy were talking about The Talking Egg before school started. They were sitting on the swings in

56

the playground looking over the column Randy had written the night before.

"I can't help it!" Randy snapped. Her cheeks were pink with anger and embarrassment. "I know Starr is awful, but there's no need to make fun of her in front of the whole school! You said you'd gather the gossip and I could write the column. Well, this *is* the column. It's the gossipy-est I'm going to write. So you'd better get used to it!"

Jamie stared at her friend in amazement. She'd never heard Randy sound so mad before. It was a little scary.

"Okay, Ran," she said meekly.

"Good." Randy still sounded stern. "And don't you go changing it all around, either!"

"Okay, Ran," Jamie said again. "I'll just take it up to the newspaper office now. I won't change it — I promise."

Randy held out the sheet of pink notebook paper. "I'll see you in class," was all she said.

Jamie walked up the stairs toward the newspaper office feeling horrible. I don't think Randy's ever yelled at me before! she thought. Well, I won't change the column. Not even one word. Not even if Cass O'Brian hates it.

Not even if she hates it, and she yells at

me, and says she knew she couldn't trust fourth-graders, and refuses to let us try again, and reads it aloud to all the other editors, and they all roar with laughter . . .

Jamie was starting to walk more and more slowly. The newspaper office was just around the corner now. *Now* it was a few feet away. And now, for some reason, Jamie's feet were taking her right past it. They walked her down the hall into the girls' bathroom, where she sat down on a bench to read the column again.

It's just not right, she told herself. Cass *will* laugh at us — and really, wouldn't Randy hate that even more than my changing a few words here and there?

Of course she would!

Jamie pulled out her pen. She wouldn't really *change* anything — only add to what Randy had already written. Randy probably wouldn't even notice. And if she did, she'd probably thank Jamie for being such a thoughtful friend.

"I can hardly believe I was lucky enough to find this," said Miss Duni in a reverent voice. She was standing next to Jamie's desk, running her hands admiringly over an old-fashioned ox yoke. "I was driving past an antique store yesterday when I suddenly saw it sitting out on the porch! I just *slammed* on the brakes. This will be perfect for your maple syrup skit, don't you think? And once I find a big pot for the sap, we'll be all set!"

Jamie glanced around helplessly. Everyone else was rehearsing their skits for the Nature's Bounty show. Larry Berman was wearing a big, bulky eggplant costume made of purple vinyl. He was practicing some kind of square dance with Leesa Alexander, who was dressed as a brussels sprout. Near them, Judy Gollin was pretending to be an apple falling off a tree. She did it by rolling off the edge of her desk. "Ow!" she yelled each time she hit the ground. And in a far corner, Mike Liu and Peter Elliot were dolefully practicing a song called "Great-Tasting Garlic."

Starr Stuart was nowhere to be seen.

"Hey, you oxen! Get that yoke on and *mush*!" shouted Farmer Baird.

"You're not supposed to say 'mush'! That's for dogs!" Jamie objected.

"Well, I'm the farmer, and I can tell my own oxen whatever I want. And I want you to *mush*! Start pulling that sap across the field!"

Reluctantly, Jamie and Randy fitted the yoke around their necks. Then they looked down at the floor.

The dirt Miss Duni had brought in several days ago was more like mud now. It had rained that morning, and everyone had tracked in water. Now there were mud and puddles everywhere.

"Are — are we supposed to crawl around in this?" Randy quavered.

"Of course you are!" Bill said heartily. "Oxen *like* getting dirty!"

Jamie and Randy looked at each other and sighed. Then they dropped onto their hands and knees and gingerly began crawling through the mud.

The yoke was heavy. It probably would have been heavy even for oxen. On two fourth-graders, it was like having a bridge draped across their shoulders.

"Come on! *Pull* that sap!" Bill shouted, cracking an imaginary whip in the air. "There won't be any food all winter if you don't — " Abruptly he broke off. "Hey, Keenan! You're slowing down! I can't have an ox with that kind of attitude! Don't forget that my parents are coming to this show! Randy, get up. I want Keenan to pull the sap all by herself today."

"No, I can't let her do — " Randy began. But Bill had already unhooked her side of the yoke.

60

"You can have a vacation in the pasture," he said. "You look kind of tired anyway. But you better get going, Keenan! You're the most pathetic ox I've ever seen!"

"Well, I guess we won't have any problems deciding who's going to be the subject of the next Talking Egg column," Jamie said grimly to Randy at recess.

Randy stared at her. "Who are you talking about?"

"*Who?* I can't believe you need to ask! Farmer Baird, of course!"

"Oh, no, Jamie. That's not a good idea at all," Randy said immediately. "He was really nice to me this morning!"

Jamie stared at her openmouthed. "But what about the way he treated *me*?" she finally asked.

"Well, maybe you just got on his nerves or something," Randy said.

"Randy, I can't believe this! Don't you *mind* getting dirty? What's wrong with you? If I didn't know better, I would swear you liked Bill the Pill or something!"

Randy blushed. "Don't — don't be silly, Jamie! It's bad enough that we're spying on people, but then making fun of them too . . . Well, I just don't like it."

"Randy, you're not being a good journalist!"

Jamie protested. "We're supposed to be professionals! Real reporters don't worry about hurting people's feelings!"

"Maybe I'm not a real reporter, then." Randy's voice was troubled. "I don't even know if I want to — "

The interruption could not have come at a worse time.

"Extra! Extra! Hot off the presses! The latest issue of The Laughing Egg Times!"

The two girls turned to see a fifth-grader standing on the school steps with a stack of papers in her hands. From all over the playground, kids came rushing toward her.

"Oh. Here's our column," Randy said listlessly. "Do you want to read it?"

Suddenly Jamie remembered what she'd been dreading all morning. It was Randy's reaction to the changed version of The Talking Egg.

"Not really, Randy," she said quickly. "Wouldn't you like to go on the swings or something? Or we could take a walk way, way across to the other side of the playground — "

"I can't *believe* this!" she heard a girl next to them say with a shocked giggle. Jamie turned quickly — and her heart sank. The girl was reading The Talking Egg.

"Starr Stuart is going to faint when she

sees this!" the girl squealed. "Kathy, come over here a second! I have to show you something!"

"Well, how about that walk, Ran?" Jamie said. "Shall we — "

"May I have a look at that paper for a second?" Randy interrupted. She was talking to the girl next to Jamie.

"Sure. But give it right back, okay?"

Jamie didn't have to peek over Randy's shoulder to know what her friend was reading.

THE TALKING EGG

Can there possibly be a girl who cares more about her looks than Starr Stuart? As a matter of fact, does she care about *anything* besides her looks? The Talking Egg doesn't think so. But we were surprised to see that Starr's beautiful blond hair is fake. She has it bleached at the Talking Egg Beauty Nest. Too bad about that little accident at the Beauty Nest yesterday, Starr. We're looking forward to seeing your new hairstyle today . . . and so is Peter Burbank. He may not know it, but Starr has singled him out as the boy of her dreams. Is it true love at last? We'll have to wait and see, but at least she's found someone good-looking enough for her. The question is: Will he have to dye HIS hair, too? The Talking Egg promises to keep you posted.

Randy's eyes were blazing. "How could you do this?" she hissed. "You *promised*, Jamie!"

"I — I know, but — "

"But nothing," Randy said. "You didn't even think about my feelings — or Starr's. Did *she* deserve this?"

"Randy, it's just a newspaper article!"

"Right. And you're just a reporter doing your job. Well, from now on you can do your job alone, Jamie. I'm finished with this stupid newspaper!"

And Randy stormed away across the playground.

Chapter Seven

Jamie had been sure she could persuade Randy to write a column about Bill once Randy cooled off. But she didn't get a chance to talk about it the next morning before school. And when class started, Miss Duni's news drove the newspaper right out of Jamie's head.

"You're not going to *believe* what I've arranged for us!" Miss Duni said when the class was sitting down. "A field trip to an actual *field*!"

"Oh, my!" said Leesa Alexander politely. "Won't that be a treat!"

"Well, we're not really going to *study* the field, although we'll be standing right in it," Miss Duni went on. "We're going to be visiting a pumpkin farm. Just perfect for fall!" She smiled radiantly.

"But Halloween was *last* month!" protested Jamie.

"Now, Jamie, the Pilgrims ate pumpkins, didn't they? They weren't concerned about Halloween being over, and you shouldn't be, either!"

Just then the classroom door opened, and Starr Stuart stalked in. She marched to her desk and sat down without looking at anyone.

There was a terrible silence.

"Why, Starr," said Miss Duni at last, "what an attractive and unusual hairstyle, dear!"

Starr had obviously decided *not* to have her hair dyed black. It was streaked, smeared, and stained with black, red, and brown — it looked like a feather headdress!

Obviously Starr wasn't going to be doing any modeling for a long, long time.

Well! thought Jamie. I guess I took care of *her*!

But she didn't really feel that proud of it. In the pit of her stomach, a little voice was whispering to her, "This time you've gone too far."

As if she could hear the little voice — and agreed with it — Randy turned and frowned at Jamie. "That was *mean*!" she said under her breath.

66

"Oh, it'll grow out," Jamie muttered. But she knew that Randy was right.

Miss Duni cleared her throat. "We missed you yesterday, dear," she said to Starr.

"I didn't want to come to school," Starr said flatly.

"I don't blame you one bit," Miss Duni blurted out. Then she seemed to catch herself. "Did you decide that you should be Indian corn in the play, instead of regular corn? What a perfectly lovely idea! Anyway, it's great that you got here in time for the field trip," she continued. "Because I think the bus is waiting for us. C'mon, gang! Let's get out there and *meet those pumpkins!*"

The ride wasn't as much fun as field trip rides usually were. Jamie and Randy sat together, but neither of them said much. That gave them the chance — not that they *wanted* the chance — to hear Starr and Judy Gollin arguing in the seat ahead of them.

"Of *course* you told The Talking Egg about my hair!" Starr was saying angrily. "Who else was in there with us?"

"Starr, I know what it looks like — but I promise I didn't say anything!" Judy answered in a tearful voice. "Why would I do something like that?"

"Why *did* you do something like that? Because you're jealous of me, that's why!"

"I am not," Judy replied. "I like you, but I — I don't want to be like you!" She sounded almost surprised at herself. "And I don't know how that stuff got into the paper — but if you think I'd do something like that, you don't know what a good friend I am! And besides, your life isn't ruined just because your hair looks funny!" she finished in a rush. "Maybe if you don't get the chance to be a model for awhile, you'll be less stuck-up!"

For the rest of the ride, Starr and Judy were as silent as Jamie and Randy.

"Are you Mr. Foley?" Miss Duni asked the old man standing in front of the roadside country store. A sign over the store's front door said, "Welcome to Little Vermont!"

"That's me," the old man replied.

"Good. I'm Miss Duni, from Laughing Egg Elementary School. I'd like to show my class your pumpkin farm."

The old man peered at her with a puzzled expression on his face. "We've had about three frosts in the last week. There aren't many good pumpkins left. Most of 'em are rotted."

"Never mind," said Miss Duni. "Well, since we've come all this way, I think it would be nice to see the pumpkins anyway.

I'm sure the class will still get a lot out of it."

Mr. Foley shook his head. "Okay," he said. "But I think it's kind of a shame you *did* come all this way. 'Sides, you won't all fit into my truck — and it's a long walk."

It was a very long walk, through three fields of dried-up cornstalks. And it seemed even longer because Bill Baird tripped Jamie about fifteen times on the way.

"Well, here we are," said Mr. Foley at last. He pointed to a field filled with muddy pumpkins on withered yellow vines. "Help yourselves."

"Oh, don't these look nice," said Miss Duni after a second. "And I'm sure there are plenty for everyone. Just pick as many as you can carry, people! We'll pay for them back at the store!"

"No charge," said Mr. Foley tersely. "As I said, they're mostly rotted."

He was right.

"Isn't this great," Jamie muttered under her breath a few minutes later as she stumbled along through the mud. "We get to be all dirty looking for rotten pumpkins that no one even — "

"Stop talking to yourself, pumpkin-head!" came a voice behind her. Jamie turned to see Bill Baird standing right at

69

her heels. He grinned and pointed to a pumpkin that was so rotted it looked like a deflated balloon. "Here's a nice one for you to take home," he said.

He scooped up a big, sticky handful of rotted pumpkin-gunk and hurled it at Jamie. With a *thwack!* it hit her on the shoulder.

For a second Jamie was paralyzed with rage. Then she scooped up a handful of the pumpkin, leaped forward, and smeared it all over Bill's face.

"Hey, no fair!" he said angrily. He bent down and scooped up another handful of mushy pumpkin — but Jamie was ready with *another* handful — and then Bill ground some into her hair — and Jamie was reaching for some more — when Bill tripped her and she fell face-first into what was left of the rotten pumpkin. And there was quite a lot of it left.

Unfortunately, Jamie wasn't able to go inside Mr. Foley's store with the other kids. She was so covered with rotten pumpkin that Miss Duni wouldn't let her. "Maybe one of your friends can bring you some maple-walnut fudge candy," Miss Duni said crossly. "I think you'd better wait on the bus. I'll spread some newspapers under you

to protect the seats."

It was half an hour before the class had finished shopping. By the time they got out to the bus, the pumpkin all over Jamie had really ripened. No one would sit with her.

Being sticky on newspapers had to be one of the worst feelings in the world. Every time Jamie moved, the papers shifted and moved along with her. But that didn't bother her half as much as watching Randy and Bill laughing together a few seats ahead of her.

It was true that when Randy had gotten on the bus, there had been only one seat left — next to Bill. But did Randy have to look so excited about it? Did she have to talk to him at all? Why wasn't she mad at him for being so mean to her best friend?

And what were they talking about so happily? And why had Randy glanced back at Jamie just then?

They're talking about me, Jamie thought. I just know it.

Then she remembered The Talking Egg. Maybe sitting on newspaper made her think of it. At any rate, Jamie's spirits lifted instantly.

I can get revenge on Bill this afternoon! she thought. All I have to do is take a shower in the locker room, put on my sneakers, turn invisible, follow him around, and ruin his life forever.

But that's not exactly how things happened.

It all went the way Jamie had planned — except that after school, Bill took his books and strolled out to a big tree on the playground.

And Randy was waiting for him under the tree.

Chapter Eight

Randy smiled demurely up at Bill. "Hi," she said as he dropped down next to her. "I thought you'd never get here!"

Jamie felt as though she'd been kicked in the stomach. Randy and Bill *liked* each other! How could they do this to Jamie? It was *treason*!

And if Randy's a traitor, Jamie suddenly thought, then I have a perfect right to spy on her.

Jamie was standing about ten feet away from the tree. Now, without hesitation, she raced over, scrambled up the trunk, and perched on a big branch where she'd be able to overhear everything.

"What was *that*?" Bill asked.

"I guess it was a squirrel," said Randy.

"Sounded more like a dog, if you ask me!"

Randy giggled as though Bill had said something really funny.

"Now," Randy went on. "Did you bring your notebook?"

"Yup. It's right here," said Bill. He pulled out a battered spiral notebook covered with ballpoint drawings of robots. "Okay," he said in a businesslike way. "So the oxen come up pulling this big vat. Should we have real syrup in the vat?"

"Well, how about just some water?' Randy suggested. "It would be horrible if there was real syrup and it spilled and we got all sticky. I know you didn't mean to get Jamie all sticky today," she added hastily.

Oh, Randy, Randy, Jamie mourned silently. Of *course* he meant to! How can you betray me this way?

"Have you seen Jamie, by the way?" asked Randy. She glanced around nervously.

"Yeah. I saw her going home," Bill said. "So then what does the farmer say?"

"Well . . ." Randy thought for a minute. "What if the farmer says his family will starve unless he can get this sap boiled into syrup?"

"Starve without maple syrup?" Bill objected. "Maple syrup's not a food! If they're starving, why doesn't he stop making syrup and go out hunting? Hey! Maybe that's a good idea! He throws the vat down on the ground and says 'My family needs meat. I'm going out hunting.' Then he gets his gun, and — "

"But this skit's supposed to be about maple syrup!" Randy broke in. "Miss Duni didn't say anything about hunting!"

"Oh, that's right," Bill said reluctantly. Then he brightened. "But of course the farmer still carries his gun with him wherever he goes."

Of *course* he does, Jamie said to herself. You'd never let him just be a nice, regular farmer. No, he has to be a gun-toting animal-killer.

Randy looked around nervously again. "I don't know why, but I keep thinking Jamie's around somewhere."

"Why are you so worried about that moron, Keenan, anyway?" Bill asked. "I don't know why you like that Brillo-head. She's a total pain."

"Oh, she's not really a pain," answered Randy in a troubled voice. "She — um — she just gets a little upset about things once in awhile."

Great. Some defense of your best friend. So I'm "not really a pain?" That's a big endorsement! Jamie fumed.

"Anyway, I want to talk about the play,

not Jamie," Randy added.

For the next half hour, that's all she and Bill did. Their ideas came faster and faster, and Jamie could tell that they were both having a great time. They didn't even seem to notice that the things they were dreaming up were utterly different.

"And then maybe this big storm comes up, and lightning knocks the tree down onto the farmer . . ." said Bill.

"And then he looks around and sees this poor orphan rabbit and decides to feed it some syrup . . ." said Randy.

"Indians attack while he's pinned to the ground! They steal the boiling syrup!" said Bill.

"And the rabbit turns out to be a fairy in disguise, the kind that can grant wishes . . ." said Randy.

"A gunshot rings out! A bowstring twangs! The farmer is shot full of arrows, but he manages to save the syrup!"

"He wishes for everyone to love maple syrup as much as he does! And it's such a nice, unselfish wish that the fairy gives him great wealth into the bargain!"

Randy and Bill smiled at each other. "It's going to be a great skit," said Randy.

"My parents will love it," Bill agreed. "They're really excited about seeing me be the lead."

"It's getting late," Randy said regretfully. "I'd probably better head home."

"I'll walk you," said Bill.

And I will, too, thought Jamie.

She waited until Randy and Bill were about twenty feet away, so that they wouldn't hear the tree rustling as she climbed down. Then she raced up behind them — so close that she could have pinched Bill if she'd wanted to. And she *did* want to, except that it would have given her away.

No, pinching Bill would be too obvious, Jamie thought. But I *can* untie his shoelace.

Quickly she knelt down and untied the lace on his sneaker. I might as well undo both of them while I'm at it, she thought. Too bad Bill is walking, or I'd be able to tie them together.

She did give one of the laces a good strong yank, though. Bill stumbled and pitched forward onto his knees.

"Ow!" he yelped as he pushed himself back up. "Did you feel that? I think it was an earthquake!"

"It was no earthquake," Randy said grimly. She whirled around. "Now, Jamie, I *know* you're there," she said, glaring into the air. "Just cut it out! Leave us alone!"

Bill stared at her in astonishment. "Is

this part of the play, too?" he asked.

Randy didn't answer him. She was still frowning fiercely in the general direction of Jamie's left shoulder. "So you're not going to say anything?" she asked. "Well, okay for you! See if I care!"

Suddenly she seemed to remember that Bill was there. "Oh! Sorry, Bill," she said. "Uh, yes. It was an idea I had for the play. But I think it would be a little too complicated to do onstage."

Bill was still staring at her. "I think so, too," he said after a second.

The two of them began walking toward Randy's house again. And it was a good thing they did — because the second after that, the magic suddenly wore off, and Jamie reappeared. Fortunately they didn't turn around, so Jamie was able to stomp home without being seen.

"Hey, Jamie, why are you stomping around like that?" asked Tim as Jamie walked through the front door. He was doing a puzzle in the living room with Mrs. Keenan. "*Bong-bong-bong!* You sound like a rhinoceros!"

"I'm not a rhinoceros. I'm an ox," she said sourly. "An ox who's just lost her best friend."

"What do you mean, honey?" asked Mrs. Keenan.

Jamie sighed heavily. "My *former* best friend, Miss Randy Dowell, has decided she likes my worst enemy better than me. Her new best friend is Bill the Pill Baird."

Without waiting for an answer, she bong-bong-bonged up the steps and into her room and flung herself down at her desk.

"Okay, Randy," she said between clenched teeth. "If you like Bill the Pill so much, I'm sure you want the whole school to know about it. You said you didn't want to write the column. You said you didn't want the column to be about Bill. Hey, no problem! *I'll* write the column — and it won't be about Bill the Pill, Ran. It'll be about *you*."

Chapter Nine

Randy was waiting at the front door of the school the next morning when Jamie got there. "How could you do this to me?" she cried the instant she saw Jamie.

Uh-oh, thought Jamie. I guess they've passed out the latest issue of The Laughing Egg Times already.

"Uh, hi, Ran," she said, heading swiftly for her locker. But Randy stayed in step right beside her.

"How could you do it, Jamie?" she repeated. "How could you follow me around like that and write about me and be such a horrible mean *spy*?" She flapped the newspaper in Jamie's face.

Jamie didn't have to look to know which page Randy was talking about. She remembered what she'd written very well. After all, she had made Betsy drive her back to school late yesterday afternoon so that she could drop it off at the newspaper office. And Cass O'Brian had praised her for meeting deadlines.

THE TALKING EGG

Anyone with two eyes can see that Randy Dowell is in love. That's because she spent yesterday afternoon out on the playground with none other than Bill "The Pill" Baird. What did they talk about? Maple syrup. A sweet subject — for a sweet couple! And things got even sweeter when The Pill walked The Traitor home after their "study" session. Why is Randy a traitor? She knows perfectly well . . . but you'll have to ask The Talking Egg if *you* want to find out.

Randy's eyes were brimming with tears of rage. "This is the worst thing you've ever done!" she shouted. They had reached Jamie's locker by now. Randy pointed down at the magic pink sneakers, which were lying half-hidden at the bottom of the locker. "You put those on and followed me around, didn't you? I'll never forgive you, Jamie!"

"You brought it on yourself," said Jamie in a dignified voice — which was hard, because her locker was so messy that books kept on falling out. "Throwing yourself at Bill Baird like that! Why, I never heard of such a — "

"Oh, shut up!" Randy interrupted crossly. "You sound like a prissy old lady. Anyway, *I* never heard of someone spying on her best friend!"

"It wasn't spying!" said Jamie just as a big pile of folders slithered out of her locker onto the floor. Fiercely she shoved them back inside. "It was research for the column! It's not *my* fault if you happened to decide to moon around all afternoon with the person the column was supposed to be about!"

"Listen to the big reporter!" jeered Randy. "You think you're such a professional — but you're really just a sneak!"

And Randy turned and stomped away down the hall toward the classroom.

"*Oh!*" Jamie whirled around and kicked her locker door as hard as she could. From inside, she could hear every book on the top shelf come thudding down to the floor.

It's all Randy's fault! she thought hotly. *She* started this! I'm *not* a sneak!

But I would hate it if some invisible person was following *me* around. . . .

But Randy *made* me follow her around!

She wouldn't help with the story! I had to do it all myself!

But the reason she wouldn't help was because she thought it was too mean . . . *Was* it too mean?

At last Jamie reached her classroom — and froze in the doorway.

Randy had traded desks with Starr Stuart. She was sitting in Starr's old seat across the room from Jamie, and Starr was just putting her stuff into what had been Randy's desk.

"Oh, hello, Jamie," said Miss Duni. "Come in, dear! We're just switching things around a little here. Randy says that she can't see the blackboard from the back of the room."

Slowly Jamie stumbled through the dirt on the floor and took her seat. Out of the corner of her eye she could see Starr's horrible-looking hair.

I wonder if Randy's trying to make me feel guilty, she thought. Well, it's not going to work!

For once it was a relief to have Miss Duni interrupt Jamie's thoughts. "I've got good news for everyone!" she trilled. "This morning Bill brought me a copy of the script he and Randy wrote for their skit. And it's very, very good. In fact, thanks to Bill's and

Randy's cooperation, the maple syrup skit is the best in the class. That's why I've chosen it to be the final number in the Nature's Bounty show at the Thanksgiving Assembly."

Miss Duni didn't mention Jamie at all.

"So there, Keenan," said Bill. And at her new desk, Randy smiled secretly to herself. Then she leaned back and whispered something to Judy Gollin, who was sitting behind her. She gestured toward Jamie and giggled. With a broad grin, Judy nodded agreement. *What are they saying about me*? Jamie wondered miserably.

"And then I dust everything *very, very* carefully," said Leesa Alexander.

It was lunchtime — and this was the very first lunch Jamie had ever eaten without Randy. Randy was laughing and talking with a bunch of girls at another table. Jamie was sitting with Leesa Alexander. That was the only place she could find a seat. And for the whole lunch period, Leesa had been talking about her special room-cleaning system.

Jamie couldn't help looking over at Randy's table. Randy was talking to another girl and giggling. When she saw Jamie, she tossed her head and turned her chair away.

"Want some split pea salad?" Leesa asked, pulling a wide mouthed Thermos out of her pink-flowered lunchbox. "I made it all by myself."

"Uh — no, thanks," Jamie muttered. "I'm not really hungry."

It didn't get any better at recess.

When the recess bell rang, Leesa made Jamie help her clean all the crumbs off the lunch table. By the time Jamie got outside, Randy was already playing Chinese jumprope with Starr Stuart and Judy Gollin. The three of them glanced in Jamie's direction for a second — and then went back to their game.

"She's always trying to horn in on everything," Jamie heard Randy say.

Jamie turned on her heel and went back into school.

The rest of the afternoon dragged along. Jamie had never been so glad to hear the last bell ring. Before Miss Duni had finished saying goodbye, Jamie was out the door.

She raced toward her locker. I can't wait to get out of here, she thought feverishly as she turned the combination on her lock. I'll go home and turn on the TV and just veg out until I can — What was the matter with her locker? It looked different, somehow, as if someone had rearranged it. The books and folders were stacked neatly on the shelves . . .

And Jamie's magic pink sneakers were gone!

Jamie stared at the floor of her locker as if she might somehow see the sneakers if she just looked hard enough. They still weren't there — but a note was. A note on pink paper. Jamie picked up the note with a sinking heart.

" 'You always said I should give them a try,' " she read aloud in a shaky voice.

The note was signed "Randy."

Chapter Ten

The sneakers will never work on Randy, Jamie told herself over and over. We don't even wear the same shoe size! I have nothing to worry about.

But somehow Jamie couldn't make herself believe it.

"Jamie, why do you keep looking around like that?" asked Margaret that night at supper. "You keep sort of hunching up and peeking around behind you as if someone were reading over your shoulder. It's really queer-looking."

"I didn't realize I was offending Your Majesty," Jamie said loftily. Making sure not to hunch up, she took a bite of pot roast. Then she froze.

"*Wait!*" she gasped with her mouth full. "*What was that clicking sound?*"

The whole Keenan family stared at her. "Didn't you hear the front door opening?" asked Jamie. She leaped up from her chair and rushed to the front hall.

The door was closed.

Slowly Jamie returned to her seat. "There's no one there after all," she said.

All afternoon she'd been sure an invisible Randy was following her. As she walked home, she had felt a little breeze on the back of her neck. Was it Randy? When Jamie walked inside the house, had Randy followed her? Had Randy been sitting next to her while Jamie ate her snack — or didn't eat it, actually, because she was so sure Randy *was* sitting next to her and listening to her chew?

"What a bundle of nerves you are," Margaret remarked. "I feel as though I'm sitting across from a pile of jello."

"Wow! This is great pot roast!" Jamie said, trying to change the subject. She put another piece in her mouth.

"AAAAAH!" she shouted, and spit the piece of meat into her napkin. "Mom! Someone's trying to salt me to death! There's a ton of salt on this meat!" She glared accusingly at her sisters. "Which one of you is trying to murder me?"

"What are you talking about, dear?" Mrs.

89

Keenan asked. "No one's touched that meat but you!"

And Randy . . .

Now Jamie was sure Randy was in the room with her. Randy must have dumped salt all over her plate while she was out of the room! Well, I'm not going to let her get to me! Jamie thought fiercely. Calmly she raised a forkful of mashed potatoes to her lips . . .

. . . and watched in horror as they flew through the air and landed with a *thwap*! in her father's left eye. An invisible Randy had just grabbed her fork and turned it into a slingshot.

"My — my fork must have slipped. I'm sorry, Dad," Jamie stammered.

Her father regarded her coldly out of his un-potatoed eye. "I should hope so," he said. "I think you've had enough to eat, Miss Keenan. You may be excused."

When Jamie trudged wearily into her classroom the next morning, the paper was already lying on her desk. It had been carefully folded open to The Talking Egg column. Obviously Randy had wanted to make sure Jamie saw it right away.

THE TALKING EGG

It's funny how some kids just can't outgrow their fear of the dark. Take Jamie Keenan, for example. Is there any other fourth-grader in this school who actually pokes around under her bed with a yardstick to check for monsters before she goes to sleep? The Talking Egg paid a surprise visit to the Keenans' house yesterday afternoon and learned many other facts about Jamie that are kind of — well — pathetic. Like the way Jamie handles a fork — so badly that she almost blinded her father at supper. Or the way she brushes her teeth — tilting her head to one side and smiling at her reflection like a model. Or the way she screamed out "MOMMY!" when she heard a tapping noise on her window. Jamie would probably say her nerves were on edge — but what The Talking Egg says is, her nerves wouldn't *be* on edge if she didn't have such a guilty conscience. About what? Keep reading, and one of these days, The Talking Egg will tell you.

Jamie threw the newspaper down and buried her head on her desk. It's war, then, she thought. Total war.

Mike Liu and Peter Elliot came trooping in. Both were carrying copies of The Laughing Egg Times, and both grinned when they saw Jamie.

"Oooooooooooooo!" Peter said in a ghostly voice. "I think there's a scary monster under your desk, Jamie! Better call your mommy!"

"Are you talking about that silly newspaper?" Miss Duni asked. "What a lot of fuss about nothing! I must say, I *do* resent the way all of you waste so much energy on outside topics instead of concentrating on nature the way you should. But since the three of you are here early, perhaps you might give me a hand." Miss Duni held up a brown paper bag that was pulsing strangely, as if something inside was alive.

"I bought a pint of earthworms from a bait shop on the way to school this morning," said Miss Duni proudly. "I thought we could put them in the dirt in the corner and see if they'd help our crops grow any faster. Why don't the three of you take a few handfuls and sprinkle them around?"

That certainly drove all thoughts of Randy out of Jamie's head — for the next few minutes, at least. But when the bell rang,

Randy wasn't in her seat.

That's strange, Jamie mused. Randy is *never* late. I wonder. . . . she's not *still* invisible, is she?

How could she be? For Jamie, the sneakers' magic always wore off in a couple of hours! But what if the magic somehow worked differently for Randy?

And what if Randy was standing behind Jamie right now?

Nervously Jamie twisted around in her seat and came face to face with Bill Baird. He flared his nostrils horribly when she caught his eye.

Jamie quickly turned back around in her seat, but she couldn't stop wondering whether Randy was standing at her elbow.

"You seem rather restless today, Jamie," Miss Duni said suddenly. "Would you please come up to the blackboard, dear?"

Oh, no, Jamie thought. She pushed her chair back and walked carefully up through the dirt to the front of the room, trying not to step on any worms that might have strayed out of the corner.

"Why don't you take notes on what I'm saying?" asked Miss Duni. "That might help you to concentrate."

Jamie actually felt relieved at her assignment. Randy wouldn't have the nerve to do something to her in front of the whole class, would she?

But when Jamie picked up a piece of chalk, she couldn't seem to keep her hand from jiggling. The chalk shook so badly that her notes never got much farther along than a few wavy lines.

Was Randy holding the chalk? Or was Jamie so nervous that she couldn't control her hand?

"You know, Jamie," Miss Duni said, "I'm not sure that your notes are working out right. Why don't you finish them later?"

Jamie put the chalk down and went back to her seat. "We'll work on the skits for Nature's Bounty instead," said Miss Duni. Then she sighed. "Yes, Jamie?"

"But Miss Duni, Randy's not here!" Jamie said. "We can't rehearse without her!"

"Good heavens, you're right!" said Miss Duni. "I never even noticed that she was missing!" She frowned thoughtfully. "That's strange. No one called in to say Randy wasn't going to be here this morning. I wonder if there's something wrong. . . . I think I'll just run down to the office to check. Stay in your seats, everyone, and be quiet."

Of course everyone — except for Larry and Leesa — started talking the instant she was out the door.

94

In the general commotion, no one noticed when Bill Baird grabbed Jamie's shoulder and squeezed it as hard as he could.

"You know where Randy is, don't you?" he growled threateningly.

"Ouch! What are you talking about?" Jamie gasped, trying to twist away. "Why would I know where she is?"

"Because she's your best friend — or she was!" said Bill. His grip on Jamie's shoulder tightened painfully.

"Listen, Keenan," he hissed. "I *know* you've done something with her. But you'd better tell me where she is. I want our skit to be the best. And the only way that's going to happen is if *all* of us are here. If you don't bring Randy back, I'll report you to the principal. Then I'll pulverize you."

Chapter Eleven

As Jamie stared at Bill in amazement, he actually clenched his fist and held it up in her face.

"Go ahead and pulverize me," she told him scornfully. "I don't know where Randy is. What do you think I am — some kind of kidnapper?"

"Maybe," Bill drawled. "Here's the way I see it. You're jealous of Randy because she comes up with a great idea for our skit. You're so jealous that you play a nasty trick on her — and then she disappears. What do *you* think that looks like, hmmmmmm? It looks as though you're trying to get Randy out of the way before the Thanksgiving Assembly!"

"Can't everybody please be *quiet*?" Larry Berman asked before Jamie could say anything. He was bouncing up and down in his seat with nervousness. "I'm sure I hear Miss Duni coming back! She'll be very disappointed in us!"

Miss Duni reappeared in the room.

"What's happened to Randy?" Bill asked.

"Well, I don't *know* what's happened," said Miss Duni with a perplexed frown. "The office secretary hadn't heard anything from Randy's parents. Maybe she's on her way. Now, why don't we take out our social studies books and . . ."

Jamie didn't hear the rest of what Miss Duni said. All of a sudden she was worried about Randy.

I don't care about getting pulverized, she thought. But what if something bad *has* happened to Randy? What if — oh, no! — what if someone *did* kidnap her?

Well, how could they? Jamie's other half asked her sensibly. You can't kidnap someone invisible!

Well, what if a car hit her or something, and she's lying invisible by the side of the road? Or what if she was walking along a train track, and suddenly she slipped, and now she's stuck on the track?

But why would Randy — of all people — be walking on a train track? asked Jamie's other half. She's much too careful to do something crazy like that!

But now Jamie was too wound up to listen to her other half at all.

It's all my fault! she thought mournfully. If only I'd been nicer, Randy wouldn't be lying helpless on a train track now, with the train whistling toward her . . . It was too awful to think about. "Miss Duni," Jamie burst out, "may I make a phone call? It's an emergency. I — I need to call home right away." It wasn't really a lie. She *did* need to call home — Randy's home.

"All right, dear, but hurry back," said Miss Duni. "And don't run in the hall!"

But Jamie was already running. She dashed all the way to the pay phone, shoved her quarter into the slot, and punched in Randy's number.

Randy's mother answered on the second ring. "Hello, Mrs. Dowell?" Jamie panted. "It's Jamie. Is — is Randy there?"

"Why, no. Isn't she at school with you?"

"Well, I haven't seen her," said Jamie truthfully.

"Oh, dear! Randy left for the bus at the usual time this morning. I wonder if something's wrong?" said Mrs. Dowell.

"Could you see her all right?" asked Jamie.

There was a little pause. "What do you

mean?" asked Mrs. Dowell.

"I mean — uh — was all of her there?" asked Jamie. "Did she look — you know — solid?"

"Jamie, I don't understand what you're saying!" said Mrs. Dowell. "Randy looked just the way she always does. Now, if you'll excuse me, dear, I think I'd better try to track her down. I'm worried that she may not have gotten to school safely. Will you have her call me if you see her?"

"I sure will, Mrs. Dowell," said Jamie. "Right away."

She hung up with a sinking heart and walked draggingly back to the classroom. Something *had* happened to Randy. She was sure of it.

And whether or not it's my fault, it *is* my fault, thought Jamie in despair. It's all because of me that Randy is gone! Oh, how can I ever get her back?

"Problem all solved?" asked Miss Duni brightly when Jamie returned. "Good," she went on without waiting for Jamie to answer. "Let's turn to Chapter Five. Who would like to read aloud?"

"I would, Miss Duni!" said Leesa Alexander. She stood up and began to read in a loud voice.

"Geography is more interesting than it

sounds. And even if it *isn't* interesting, we must learn the geography of the world around us. For example, U. S. citizens must know the names of the fifty states — even the states only a few people live in, such as—"

Suddenly a shocked-looking Randy was standing in the front of the room. There was a buzz of astonishment from the class.

Quickly Jamie checked out Randy's feet. Yes, Randy was wearing the pink sneakers. That meant she'd been invisible all along.

And probably snooping around my desk the whole time! Jamie thought crossly. She leaned back in her seat and crossed her arms. Watching Randy try to explain this was going to be fun.

"Randy!" gasped Miss Duni. "Where did *you* come from?"

"I — I — " Randy quavered.

"Miss Duni, I was looking right toward the front of the room, and she wasn't there!" said Larry Berman shrilly. "She just suddenly appeared out of nowhere! It's like a nightmare or something!"

"What's going on, Randy?" asked Miss Duni.

Randy's face was a sickly shade of white. She opened and closed her mouth a few times, but no sound came out. Then she looked weakly — helplessly — over at Jamie.

Jamie gave her a cold stare in return. I'm just going to let you suffer, she thought. You got yourself into this. Stealing things out of my locker! Sneaking around after me and writing nasty things about me . . ."

But who started that? Jamie suddenly asked herself. And she knew she couldn't leave Randy hanging.

She thought quickly — and then burst into applause. "That was perfect, Ran!" she cheered. "Miss Duni, did you see the way Randy just seemed to pop up like that? We've been working on it for days. Don't you think it'll be perfect for our skit?"

"But she *did* just pop up!" protested Larry. "She didn't just *seem* to — "

Jamie charged on. "You see, Randy was supposed to be portraying the — the spirit of the sap!" she improvised wildly. "All winter the sap is hidden in the trees, and then, when spring comes — well, suddenly it's *there!* Just the way Randy is!"

"Hey!" Bill put in. "That's not supposed to be part of the script!"

"Well, of course it may not get into the final version," Jamie said glibly. "We just wanted to try it out. Didn't we, Ran?"

"Th-that's right," Randy choked out. "Just trying it out."

"We still need to practice it a little more," Jamie added. "But can't we rehearse the skits now that Randy's here? I think we're all very eager to start thinking about crops again."

"Oh, what a good idea!" said Miss Duni immediately. "Everybody put their books away, and let's start practicing! The show's only a week away, you know!"

"Ready, Bill?" Jamie asked cheerily.

He frowned at her, and then turned to the front of the room where Randy was still standing. A perplexed frown creased his forehead. "I guess I'm ready," he said at last. "But don't you guys try any more of that popping in and out during *this* rehearsal. We're sticking to the script the way Randy and I wrote it!"

"No problem," said Jamie, and she meant it. She ran up to the front of the room toward Randy. "Take off the sneakers," Jamie whispered into her ear. "You might disappear again. The magic kind of switches on and off."

Without a word Randy did as she was told. Jamie ran back to her desk and dropped her magic sneakers under it. Then she ran back up to Randy and the two of them put on their ox horns, ears and tails before they got into the yoke.

Bill was right behind her. "C'mon, you two oxen," he said. "Let's move it! Start hauling that syrup!"

Jamie and Randy dropped down on all fours and began to crawl gingerly through the dirt.

"I can't believe you're back, Ran! How long did you stay invisible?" Jamie whispered.

No answer.

"Oh, come on. You're not still mad at me, are you?" said Jamie. "Isn't it a great feeling, being invisible? Did you try it out on your family?

No answer.

"*Move* it, oxen!" Bill Baird called out. Both girls began to crawl a little faster.

"Randy!" Jamie hissed. "Talk to me!"

"No," Randy whispered back. "I'm not speaking to you ever again!"

Jamie stopped dead in her knee-tracks. "Why not?" she demanded in her normal voice. "After I got you out of trouble?"

"Well, you only got me out of it after you got me into it!" Randy snapped. "I'm just paying you back!"

It was hard for Jamie to turn her head in the yoke, but she did the best she could as she turned to stare at Randy. "Paying me back by *stealing my sneakers*?" she shouted.

"You total pig!"

"Look who's talking about being a pig!" Randy shouted back. "*You're* the one who spits food all over the place!"

"Yes — after *you* try to poison me!"

The yoke definitely made it hard to have a good fight. Both girls were bumping around awkwardly inside it as they yelled at each other.

"Girls! Girls!" cried Miss Duni, rushing up to them. "Is this any way for oxen to behave? Now calm down!"

"She started it!" both girls said at once, looking up at Miss Duni from the dirty floor.

"She spied on me — "

"She tried to poison me — "

"She's a traitor — "

"EEEEEK! There are worms all over the floor!" Randy screamed.

"ATTENTION, PLEASE!" came a voice from the intercom.

"The editors of The Laughing Egg Times would like to see Jamie Keenan and Randy Dowell in the newspaper office. Right now."

Chapter Twelve

Startled, Jamie jumped to her feet — or tried
to. She only got halfway up before the yoke
jerked her back down. "Ow!" she yelled.
"Somebody get me out of this thing!"

"Here," said Miss Duni quickly, and un-
snapped the yoke. "All right, girls, hurry
down to the newspaper office. But don't
waste any time. The Nature's Bounty show
needs you!"

"And don't run in the halls!" she called
after them.

This time there was no need for the warn-
ing. Jamie and Randy were both walking
very, very slowly.

"Why do you suppose they want us?"
Randy quavered. "Do you think we're
fired?"

"Probably," said Jamie glumly. Good-bye,

newspaper career, she thought. Good-bye, brilliant future.

When they reached the office, Cass was waiting for them with a very stern look on her face.

"Sit down," she barked.

The girls obeyed.

Cass was sitting behind a desk covered with typed stories. Jamie could only get a glimpse of one headline: "Noise in the Halls a Problem, Teachers Say." Boy, that sounds dull, she thought. At least our column is more interesting than — Cass cleared her throat. "Kids, I'm not going to waste any time," she said.

"Don't call us kids!" Jamie said indignantly. "We're only two years younger than you are!"

"All right, then — *girls*. Girls, I don't like what's been happening in your column. At first it was great. You seemed to get gossip about stuff I never would have imagined kids your age could find. How *did* you find out all that stuff about the teachers' lounge, by the way?"

"Oh, we — we just kind of stayed out of sight," said Jamie.

"Well, that was really great reporting," said Cass. "But now — "

"Darn it!" interrupted a girl who was

sitting at the typewriter. She yanked out the piece of paper she'd been working on and threw it over her shoulder.

"Now you've started using the column to argue with each other," Cass said. "What's going on?" Jamie gave Randy a sidelong glance — and saw that Randy was doing the same to her.

"Well — " she and Randy both began at the same time.

"*This stupid typewriter!*" yelped the girl behind Cass. She yanked out another sheet of paper and tossed it over her shoulder.

Cass sighed. "What's the problem, Dawn?" she asked.

"This typewriter's the problem!" said the girl who was typing. "Why do we have to use an old manual typewriter, anyway? Why can't we have a word processor?"

"Because *real* reporters always bang out their stories on old manual typewriters," said Cass. "I've seen a lot of movies about newspapers, and I know. It's just not authentic to do it any other way. Now, kids, you were saying?" She trained her gaze on Jamie and Randy again.

"We weren't saying anything," Jamie said, a little surprised at her own boldness. "We're sorry if we were unprofessional. It won't happen again."

108

"It certainly won't," said Cass sternly. "But I don't really want to punish you, kids. You were doing a great job until you started fighting with each other. So I'm going to give each of you your *own* gossip column."

"Why?" Jamie blurted out.

"Because The Talking Egg's a big hit," Cass explained. "Everyone turns to that page first. They just don't seem to *care* about the serious news. I decided that if one Talking Egg column was good, two would be even better. Isn't that great?"

Jamie couldn't answer. She was thinking furiously.

With two columns, Randy and I could do whatever we wanted! she thought. Randy could write nice, polite stuff, and I could spy on the principal's house! Then Cass would really be impressed! I could go into the boys' locker room! I could — but why did the image of Starr Stuart's face — and her horrible multicolored hair — keep floating into Jamie's mind?

I went overboard on that story, Jamie suddenly realized. And I *know* that's not why Great-Aunt Letitia gave me the sneakers. She wanted me to have fun — not wreck people's lives. Even for my own newspaper column.

"Well?" said Cass. Jamie lifted her head.

"That's nice of you, Cass," she said steadily. "But I don't want to write any more gossip columns. Why don't you give the job to Randy?"

"No!" Randy said quickly. "*I* certainly don't want it. Jamie's the one who really deserves the job, Cass. She's the one who did all the work!"

"No, no, I'm through with gossip," said Jamie. "You were right, Randy. It's just too mean. You'd do it a lot more — more kindly."

"But you're so good at it!" said Randy. "I can't write nearly as well as you."

Cass pushed back her chair with a jerk and stood up. "Oh, for heaven's sake!" she snapped. "Let's just forget the whole thing, then! I can see that you're just not mature enough to be good reporters. Now please go. You've wasted enough of my time already."

But for once the sting in Cass's words didn't even touch Jamie. She walked out of the newspaper office feeling light and free, as though she'd dumped the whole awful quarrel with Randy at Cass's feet. Even going back to a classroom filled with mud seemed like fun now.

"Oh, Jamie, I'm sorry about everything. I should never have — " Randy began.

"It was all my fault," Jamie interrupted. "You were completely right, Ran. I *was* being too mean. And I'll never do it again."

"Well, *you* were right that I wasn't writing the column well enough," said Randy. "I guess I'm just not cut out to be a writer like you."

"Oh, I'm no writer," said Jamie. "I was just showing off. I'm really just an ox."

Both girls laughed. "Me, too. Let's go back and be the best oxen Miss Duni has ever seen!" said Randy.

Chapter Thirteen

"Who's out there?" Jamie asked nervously.

"Everyone," said Judy Gollin in a doom-filled voice as she peeked through a hole in the curtain.

Jamie had been hoping that somehow, something would happen to prevent the Thanksgiving Assembly from taking place. But the school hadn't burned down, Miss Duni hadn't quit her job, the world hadn't come to an end, and the day of the Assembly — today — had finally arrived. The show would start in ten minutes.

Behind the curtain, Miss Duni's class was getting ready, each in his own way. Starr Stuart, who was wearing a corncob costume that managed to look remarkably like a green bathing suit, was leaning against the wall and practicing the corn song Miss Duni had written for her. Somehow she'd even managed to make her multicolored hair look good.

Larry Berman and Leesa Alexander were feverishly going over their scripts, but Mike Liu and Peter Elliot were just sitting on the floor with their heads in their hands. Jamie could see how much they dreaded having to sing their duet about garlic. She didn't blame them. The entire football team was supposed to be out in the audience tonight.

Jamie gave an impatient tug to her ox tail, adjusted the papier-mâché horns on her head, and peeked out through the curtain herself. She could see her entire family sitting about halfway back, the way she'd asked them to do.

Next to Jamie's family were Randy's parents. That beautiful woman putting on lipstick in the front row had to be Starr Stuart's mother. They looked exactly alike. And there were Larry Berman's parents, his father crouching in the aisle with a video camera while his mother read the instructions aloud. And behind them were — "Hey, stop peeking through the curtain! Let *me* see out there!" Bill Baird gave Jamie a hard shove out of the way and poked his entire head through the curtain. "Hey, Dad!" he shouted.

"HELLO, SON!" Jamie heard someone bellow back. Bill's father had one of the loudest voices she'd ever heard. "LET'S GET THIS SHOW ON THE ROAD!"

"Well, I'm trying," Bill complained, "but — "

"*Bill!*" Miss Duni said in a scandalized voice. She came rushing up to Bill and pulled him away from the curtain.

Now Jamie saw that Miss Duni had taken her pilgrim costume even farther than she had in school. She was dressed from head to toe like one of the founding fathers. Knickers and a square white collar completed her incredibly authentic outfit. Miss Duni clapped her hands. "Okay, people! Let's get off the stage! I'm about to go out and greet the parents, and then the show will begin!"

"I'm going to faint!" said Leesa Alexander in a wobbly voice.

"No, you're not!" said Larry Berman. "Brussels sprouts *never* faint! They know their teacher is counting on them!"

"Y-you're right," said Leesa. "We mustn't let Miss Duni down." She allowed Larry to lead her off into the wings, and Jamie and Randy followed. Then, with an excited wave to everyone backstage, Miss Duni pushed her way through the curtain.

There was a ripple of laughter from the

audience as they saw Miss Duni's outfit. Miss Duni looked puzzled at the sound. Then her face cleared and she smiled broadly.

"Yes, Thanksgiving *does* make us laugh, doesn't it — laugh with joy," she said. "And tonight our fourth grade hopes to make you laugh with joy many times. Now, we've got all kinds of crops to share with you tonight," Miss Duni went on. "But first I'd like to share with you a little song I wrote. As some of you may know, I'm really almost a professional songwriter. This song is all about how hard it was for the Pilgrims to grow the food for that very first Thanksgiving."

She cleared her throat and began to sing in a high, piercing voice.

"Oh, the crops they were so hard to
    grow,
It made the Pilgrims worry so,
They worked and worked from morn
    till night,
But still of hunger they'd such a
    fright ..."

Miss Duni's song turned out to have about thirty verses. When at last she finished, the audience burst into hearty applause.

That's because they're glad it's over, Jamie thought.

"And now," said Miss Duni, "we'd like to introduce you to a few of the dishes at that first Thanksgiving feast. First come two special favorites of mine — eggplant and brussels sprouts."

Onto the stage rushed Larry and Leesa. It was hard for them to move because of their costumes, and probably it would have been better if Leesa hadn't tried to turn a cartwheel. She landed with a thud on her stomach. But her brussels sprout costume wasn't too badly dented, and she picked herself up with a smile.

"Hello, Mr. Purple!" she chirped to Larry. "I'm so happy and proud to be the Pilgrims' favorite vegetable!"

Larry's brow puckered with fake concern. "What, Miss Green? *You're* the Pilgrims' favorite? But everyone knows that the Pilgrims love *eggplant* more than anything else in the world!"

On and on the skit went, each line dumber than the last. Finally it ended with Larry and Leesa shaking hands and shouting "Let's go get ready for dinner!"

Next came Starr Stuart. She threw back her head and began to belt out her song.

"Oh, I am corn,
Sweet, yellow corn,
On cobs and in flakes
To wake you up in the morn . . ."

That was as far as she got before whoops and barking noises began to erupt from all over the auditorium. Starr glared out at the audience for a second, then threw up her hands and marched offstage. "They just don't appreciate talent!" she said angrily.

Jamie and Randy had to sit through eight more skits until at last Miss Duni gave them a gleaming smile and walked out onto the stage again.

"Now, for our final number we're presenting a crop that I know is a big favorite of all of ours," she said. "I'm talking about maple syrup — sweet, amber maple syrup. Of course maple syrup is really harvested in the spring, but I'm *quite* sure the Pilgrims enjoyed it at Thanksgiving too. Here, to bring you the delights of a gift from the trees, are Jamie Keenan, Randy Dowell, and Bill Baird." She threw her arm out toward the wings. "Take it away, guys!"

"Oh, Jamie, I can't go out there!" whispered Randy.

"We can do it, Ran," Jamie encouraged

her. "Don't be scared. It'll be over before you — "

But before she could finish, Bill Baird was striding out onto the stage in his farmer's costume. "GET OUT HERE, MY OXEN!" he boomed.

"Okay, Ran," said Jamie, giving Randy a quick hug. "Let's go out and knock 'em dead."

Quickly she and Randy fastened the yoke around their necks and began to crawl onstage, dragging the vat of pretend maple syrup behind them.

"Ah, here are my oxen!" Bill said. "Now we will tug the vat of syrup to the fire." He pulled off his belt and waved it viciously in the air. "Hurry up, you sluggards!"

Hey! thought Jamie. That's not in the script!

The belt whistled through the air. It didn't even come close to the girls, but it *sounded* so close that both Jamie and Randy flinched and jerked away from it. A wave of water slopped over the side of the vat all over the floor. There were scattered giggles from the audience.

"Hurry!" shouted Bill again. "Mush! You're the worst oxen I've ever seen!"

Jamie and Randy struggled across the floor toward the red construction paper fire on the other side of the stage. More and more water was spilling out of the vat as they went along. It was making the floor awfully slippery, Jamie realized.

The belt swished around through the air again. "*Bill!*" Jamie heard Miss Duni whispering fiercely as the girls strained to get out of Bill's way. "You cut that out!"

But Bill didn't seem to hear. "Faster! Faster! You oxen are really stupid!" he bellowed. And he swished the belt so wildly that Jamie leaped straight into the air.

That's when the yoke cracked in half, and the reins holding Jamie to the vat snapped in two.

Jamie sailed across the stage, skidded over the edge, and landed squarely in Mr. Baird's lap.

"HEY!" shouted Mr. Baird. "GET THIS WET OX OUT OF HERE!"

As Jamie scrambled off Mr. Baird's lap, she could hear Miss Duni frantically hissing, "Pull the curtain! *Pull the curtain!*"

The curtain whumped down, and all the lights went out.

Quickly Jamie scrambled back onto the stage and vanished behind the curtain.

"I don't want to hear about it, Bill," Miss Duni was saying tautly. "You've ruined everything. You don't *deserve* another chance."

"But Miss Duni, my parents want to see me in this skit!" Bill protested.

"Well, they'd still *be* seeing you in it if you hadn't decided to start acting like a dogsled racer!" Miss Duni snapped. For once she sounded like an ordinary, normal teacher instead of her semi-crazy self. "No, there's no way I'm putting you back on stage. You go and change into your regular clothes right now."

"But what will I tell my parents?" Bill whined.

"Tell them what a nasty bully you really are!" said Miss Duni. "I'm sure it will be very educational for them!"

As Bill dragged himself off to change, Miss Duni turned and saw Jamie. "I'm all right," Jamie said quickly, before her teacher could ask. "I just want to take this wet costume off."

Miss Duni smiled gratefully at her. "You're a good sport, dear. I'm going to step out and have a little word with the audience."

She smoothed her hair and pushed her way through the curtain, and Jamie heard the audience quieting down.

"That concludes our part of the program for this evening," Miss Duni said sweetly. "Thank you for sharing the wonders of the

Thanksgiving harvest with us. Now, some of you are probably wondering why we didn't complete the last skit. Well, that's to show you that not every crop is harvested. Sometimes, unforeseen accidents prevent us from enjoying *all* of Nature's Bounty. And now, I'd like to sing you a song of farewell . . ."

Jamie didn't bother to listen to the song. She sat down on an overturned wastebasket and began to peel off her costume.

"Jamie?" Jamie looked up to see her mother peering through the door that led backstage. "Dad and I were wondering if you and Randy would like to go out to Smucky's for ice cream. We've already checked with the Dowells, and it's fine with them if Randy wants to go."

To Jamie's relief, her mother didn't mention anything about their skit.

"Hey, that would be great!" exclaimed Jamie. "But could you do me one favor first, Mom? Could you take off my tail for me? I can't find the pin, and I don't want to walk into Smucky's with a tail."

Smucky's was everyone's favorite restaurant. As Jamie looked now, she realized that about half her class was there already.

"Well, what's everyone going to have?" asked Jamie's father. "We might as well decide while we're waiting."

"I'm having a black raspberry ice-cream cone, the way I always do," said Jamie.

"And I'll have two scoops of vanilla ice cream in a dish," said Randy.

"Just plain vanilla, dear? Do you want some kind of syrup with that?" asked Mrs. Keenan.

Both Randy and Jamie shuddered. "No, thanks," said Randy firmly. "No syrup of *any* kind."

"I don't blame you," said Margaret cheerfully. "That skit was pretty pathetic."

"Margaret!" protested Mrs. Keenan. "I think — I think both Jamie and Randy did a lovely job. At least," she corrected herself, "at least as good a job as they *could* do, considering the way that nasty Bill Baird behaved."

"I *told* you he was horrible!" Jamie said.

"Look — there he is with his parents!" Randy exclaimed.

Jamie glanced around. Yes, all three Bairds were at the end of the line, waiting for a table. And it didn't surprise Jamie to see the three of them start trying to push their way ahead of the people in front of them.

"Oh, don't worry about it, Ran," Jamie said. She lowered her voice to a whisper.

"Anyway, now that we *both* know how to use the magic sneakers, Bill Baird is in for a *lot* of trouble!"